Love
and the
Sea and
Everything
in
Between

Love and the Sea and Everything in Between

BRIAN MCBRIDE

W|G *Wilder Ground Books*

 Published by Wilder Ground Books
1830 Stony Point RD
Santa Rosa, CA 95407

This Wilder Ground Books paperback edition November 2018.

Cover photo by Jacob Walti.
Cover design © 2018 by Brian McBride.

Printed in United States of America.
ISBN-13 978-0-578-40188-1

Other works by Brian McBride:

Every Bright and Broken Thing
Sons of Slaughter

PRAISE FOR *LOVE AND THE SEA AND EVERYTHING IN BETWEEN*

"With profound clarity, powerful grace, and breathless writing, *Love and the Sea and Everything in Between* explores the ugly truth of mental illness, the transformative power of love, and the endless, beautiful expanse of life we so often find ourselves lost in." - Olivia J. Bennet, author of *A Cactus in the Valley*

"*Love and the Sea and Everything in Between* is a powerful narrative about mental illness as it takes you through a whole different path of life. Brian has written so remarkably that you get lost in the undeniable weakness we all call love." - Janelle Mainero, founder of book blog *What She Sees*

"This book was amazing. I loved every word!" - *Wattpad user @Poppypea*

"This book showed me that it's okay to be broken, so thank you. It's going to change the way people see things and that's all a writer can ever ask for. The characters were beautiful in their own ways. The writing was absolutely brilliant and the book as a whole was so inspiring. Your writing is amazing and this book was amazing. I would read it a thousand times over." - *Wattpad user @SilverMoon_78*

"This story was absolutely beautifully written. I couldn't peal myself away. It was beautifully tragic and heroic at the same time. It's changed how I view things... life. This was honestly touching to read." - *Wattpad user @mugglegirl1*

"This is one of the most beautiful books I've read." - *Wattpad user @CoralBirdy*

"This book was absolutely magnificent. It had me laughing, crying, or smiling constantly! I binge-read this story and I cannot express how thankful I am to have read this. I was recovering from depression a while ago and, of course, I still have some bad days... This story helped me through all my doubts, all my disbeliefs. Thank you for this unforgettable, incredible, wonderful, and lovely journey." - *Wattpad user @asackman*

"This book was amazing. The concept was great and it was masterfully written. It changed my view of the world and taught me to be more observant. It showed me that no matter how bleak things are, there is always hope. This book was truly stunning." - *Wattpad user @runaway99*

To my parents
who showed me the way.

To my Jesus
who gave me the strength.

PART 1

1

I think that, maybe, everyone is lost. Because I don't know how I got here. That happens a lot. And I think that, maybe, everyone is insane, taunted by the voices of a thousand different phantom faces. Ripped apart in a thousand different directions. And I think that, maybe, everyone forgets. Forgets they are alive. Forgets they exist. Forgets like I forgot a long time ago. I shout into the void that I exist, but the silence drowns me out.

Vividly, though, I recall every broken thing that has brought me to this moment. But they all seem so foreign. Like strangers on a train, I avoid eye contact. I was much better at staying hidden anyway.

The world is big and important and I suppose that means I don't matter. Because the world is too big and too important to concern itself with someone who isn't.

And I guess that's why I'm standing on the Golden Gate Bridge, staring out at the big, big world. The bay wind beats against me, pulling my flannel shirt up into the air behind me like a cape. The sky is fury and the ocean is glass, shattered by the fist of an angry god. Still, I don't think I've ever seen anything so beautiful.

My fists tighten around the cold, orange railing. The water rages below, like a bellowing beast just waiting to swallow me. I inhale sharply, breathing in the cold, early morning air. Cars fly behind me, oblivious to the thoughts that race through my mind. The day has barely begun, but here I am. This was always the plan. I have the note in my wallet to prove it. It could be over soon. I would black out before I ever hit the water. I wouldn't feel a thing. I would be another success story in the Big Book of Statistics.

But something holds me in place. As if the cold of the wind has made me into a statue of ice. Perhaps it's the sliver of orange that pierces through the gray clouds, scattering color across the dark. Strange how something so small can make your soul dance. Just a little, but just enough.

A lump forms in my throat and my eyes burn. It seems paradoxical that I could only ever feel too much or nothing at all, that there is no in-between, no middle ground. I am a walking contradiction.

The wind fights against me, as if willing me to walk away. And I almost listen. If I had to imagine how I would die, I never would've placed myself here, in a place like this. I remember every little thing that brought me here, but it's like an abstract painting in my head. Colorful and clear, but everything's in the wrong place. It's a random assortment of confusing things that somehow make sense.

I like the thrill in my heart, though. The feeling of fear as I look down at my oceanic grave. It's addicting, like the sensation of blade to skin. It's almost as if the tension between life and death that burns inside of me is the only thing that has kept me alive after all these years. The frustration between my will to live and my will to die is fuel for my soul. Perhaps it is that I am starved for feeling; or perhaps it is that I feel all too much.

And that is my dilemma. The problem changes daily; with it, so does the solution.

My hands grip the ice-cold iron of the Golden Gate Bridge's rails. I hear the sound of early-morning commuters flying past me, on their way to begin their day, oblivious that I might choose to end mine here.

Why, says the wind in front of me.

I have no good answer.

Why not, says the sea.

Again, I have no answer. I can't properly put to words the need that I have inside of me. I feel altogether too big and too small for this world and my options are so severely limited.

I see everything. Too much all at once and it all crashes together, a tangle of past, present, and future. A witch's brew of every maddening possibility. Pain mingles with fringes of hope in an unruly dance. It all feels like too much.

I exist, I remind myself. Because it's so easy to forget. It's so easy to fade. To become like... *them.*

I exist, I remind myself. Because the world is content to let me disappear. But I'm not ready. Not yet. Not like this.

I exist. I want to scream it. This lump in my throat, I want to release it. I am discontent with merely abiding by the breeze. I belong to the fathoms and fathoms of endless, relentless humanity that contend inside my soul. It's too loud in here. I'm never settled. This heart is restless, leaping in waves of reckless emotion.

I exist in leaps and bounds too big for the world to

contain. The enigma leaves me endlessly frustrated. And it seems there is no one on this earth big enough to understand me.

I put my foot on the first rung of the railing and begin to lift myself up and over until soon I'm standing on the other side, nothing between me and the bottom of the sea. My arms are twisted behind me, shaking, gripping tightly to the railing. My body doesn't want to die, but my soul might be stronger.

Louder now, the wind presses my back against the bridge, as if willing me to turn back. I wonder if any of the drivers behind me notice me. Somehow, I doubt it. No one stops for strangers anymore.

5...

I start to count.

4...

My heart races.

3...

My head pounds.

2...

My jaw tenses and I close my eyes.

1...

I scream.

2

I can't do it. I hate that I can't, but there is something inside of me that refuses to let go of the bridge. Even as I stare down at the dark, roiling bay, a step away from it all ending, I can't bring myself to do it.

What's worse is that I still want to do it.

Frustrated, I look up and scream at the sky. "Just one step and it all could've been over. You and I could've finally gone our separate ways."

The sky stares back at me with a blank expression.

With a growl, I thrust a fist toward the sky. The movement causes my foot to slip from the edge of the bridge and I almost fall, but manage to catch myself with my other hand still on the railing. Even in the middle of the panic, I see the irony of the fact that now I'm holding on for my life.

I pull myself back onto my feet and scramble back over the railing to safety. Breathless, hands on my knees, I stare back out at the water just as the sun begins to shine through, parting the fog as if it's the Red Sea.

With a sigh, I say, "Okay, then. Not today." I roll my eyes. "I hear you loud and clear."

Chewing my lip, I start to turn away, but my hand won't let go of the railing and I feel that familiar anger again rise up within me. Anger that, of all things, I couldn't even manage to accomplish this. And I feel so powerless that I can't even take control of the end of my own life.

"This isn't the end," I tell the sun.

The sun above blinks back and the ocean below just laughs.

And I swear I'm going insane.

3

I find Gus, my 1972 Volkswagon Bus, parked right where I left him at the end of the bridge. Swinging the driver's seat door wide open I see the keys right where I left them too. I slide onto the seat, put my hands on the wheel, and stare back out at the bridge for a minute. A moment later, I realize I'd been holding my breath and let out a long exhale. With a slam, I close Gus' door and slip the keys in the ignition, giving it a turn until he groans to life.

Right as I'm about to back out of the parking lot, my eyes are drawn to some graffiti scrawled on the stone wall that separates the parking lot from the steep hillside that rolls down into the bay. *I exist.*

With a smirk, I shift Gus into drive and fly out of the parking lot.

I'm late. I had no intention of ever showing up for my classes this morning, but being tardy still bothers me. I've never not shown up on time; I'm mentally incapable of it. It's a blessing and a curse.

I park Gus in front of the men's dormitory and race to my room. I don't really know why I'm still going to this school – a Bible college is honestly the last place I should be. I'm pretty sure if I stay any longer God might strike me down in a bolt of lightning. I can't leave, though. My mother would be concerned for me and start to worry and I don't want my mother to worry. She doesn't deserve that. Not from me. Not after all we've been through.

Ever since Dad left... God and I are all she has. And I know she had high hopes for me, that one day I would change the world. But right now I'm barely surviving it.

I thought that church would've been a safe place. I feel stupid for thinking I'd finally found a place to belong. How wrong I was. People only care about themselves – no matter what religion they come from.

I close the door of my dorm behind me. I was one of the lucky few who didn't get a roommate this semester, so I don't have to worry about trying to explain myself to anyone.

My bed is made neatly from early this morning before I left. On the pillow, I had placed my journal for someone to find after I was gone; that way, no one would have to wonder why I did it. But now it seems pointless. I grab it and thumb through the pages, lingering on the places where drops of blood have long since dried. I wince and wonder how I got here. How did I become this person? It's all in these pages. Every word, my innocence poured out in ink.

The last line: "I'm sorry, Mom."

My jaw tense, I look up and blink back the emotion as it attempts to escape.

Not today, I tell myself.

Blinking, I close my journal and shove it inside my backpack. I toss it over my shoulder as I make my way to the Education Building.

With one last look in the mirror to make sure I look put-together enough, I head out through the common area and back outside. The sun is bright now and I feel all too visible, like maybe it's watching me.

I slip into the Ed Building and tread the tile floors lightly so my sneakers don't attract any attention. I'm half-tempted to skip classes today. (It wouldn't be a first.) I have absolutely no desire to sit through another lecture on theology or philosophy or apologetics or math. (I hate math.)

My body makes the decision for me as I pass the door to Systematic Theology and duck inside the restroom. I lock myself inside one of the stalls and sit there, trying not to hyperventilate.

Attending a smaller school has proved problematic. There's no avoiding them; the people who left, the people who lied, the people who – maybe inadvertently – turned me into a shadow of myself. I can't ignore the jealousy that brews inside my chest when I see them. They have something I never seem to be able to hold onto. But I guess it's their right. They're not me and I'm not them.

For all I know, it took them a long time to get to this point. I try not to judge, but it's hard. Because all I want is what they have and all I see is what I don't have. *Family. Friends. Love. Success. Happiness.* Yet my own happiness continues to elude me.

I try to remember the last time I was really happy, but the memories are too far gone and they crumble to pieces in my hands like sandcastles under the pressure of the waves. Throat dry and chest pulsing, I try to control my breathing, try to calm myself down as the anxiety and wretched human emotion takes control.

You can't avoid them, I tell myself. *Don't let them win. Take control of yourself. Don't let him win.*

Sitting on the toilet, I spend more time than I should reading the graffiti on the stall door. Most of it means nothing. Not to me, anyway. I reach into my backpack and produce a sharpie of my own. I think for a second about what I want to write and when I find it, I scrawl it onto the stall door right above the lock. *I EXIST.* And I hope that maybe someone will notice.

I leave the restroom behind and carefully make my way out of the Ed Building. Classes are still in session so I don't expect to run into anyone, but better safe than sorry. I walk to the far end of the campus and slip into the narrow walkway between the dormitory building and the fence. I follow the concrete path all the way behind the building to where it widens a little to give the maintenance guy access to the power room.

Slipping my backpack off my shoulders, I sit with my back against the door so that I'm facing the train tracks on the other side of the fence. I unzip the front pouch and reach in, producing a half-empty pack of cigarettes. I light one and bring it to my lips, inhaling deeply. The smoke fills my lungs as I hold my breath, chest burning. I let it out in a slow exhale and the smoke wraps itself around me.

Drawing in another slow burn, I think back to the first time I learned what smoking was. My father sat on the front porch of our house, rocking back and forth in his rocking chair, a beer in one hand and a cigarette in the other. I looked up at him with wondering eyes as he took a swig of his beer.

"What's that?" I had asked, pointing at the cigarette innocently.

He chuckled and leaned forward, twirling the mysterious thing between his fingers. "How about you take a hit and find out?" He handed it to me.

I held it between my fingers, brow furrowed, unsure.

"Put it in your mouth and breathe it in, kid. It'll hurt at first, but you'll learn to like it."

I did what my father told me to do and he was right. It hurt. I hacked as my lungs fought against the invasion.

My father laughed and confiscated the cigarette, returning it to his own lips.

I'm brought back to the present by the familiar horn of a distant train. I feel the thunder of the steel on the earth as it draws nearer and nearer. It races by in a blur just as I return the cigarette to my lips. I let it hang there, watching each car as it passes by. I imagine for a moment what it would be like to feel the force of that train against my bones and think that one day I may have the chance to find out.

Classes are over. Lunch is over. Most of my classmates lock themselves in their dorm rooms to study, but some linger outside the dorms, talking, oblivious to the stranger making his way to his eighth counseling session. I guess I don't blame them. Not all of them, anyway. Unfair as it may be, I feel like they should know. I feel like they should see me and know what's going on. That I'm not okay.

Like I said: I know it's unfair to want that. They didn't put the knife in my hands. They didn't push me off the Golden Gate Bridge. They didn't make me go to counseling. I did it of my own free will and there's some comfort in that; knowing that some things are still within my ability to control.

When I woke up this morning, I thought I'd finally be free from having to listen to Dr. Keller drone on and on for forty-five minutes about something he couldn't possibly understand. I guess the world - or God - has a different plan for me. But I don't think they realize paying someone to judge your every move doesn't help when you already want to kill yourself.

Opening the door to the Admin Building, I'm greeted by the receptionist. "Hello," she chimes. "How are you today, Adam?"

"Well, I'm just swell today, Mrs. Ortiz," I say with a smile, donning my familiar mask of practiced charm. I'm a professional at being anyone but myself. "And how are you? How's the new baby? Is your daughter able to take her home yet?"

"Eva's doing very well. And so is her mom! Thank you so much for asking, Adam. The doctor said they should both be able to go home this week."

"That's awesome! I've been praying for you all," the words taste almost bitter in my mouth, but I know Mrs. Ortiz will appreciate the sentiment. *The things you do for others...*

"We all so appreciate it. Thank you." She smiles. "Dr. Keller should be right out. Go ahead and have a seat while you wait."

"Thanks. I know the drill," I laugh with a wink. I sit on the cold, stiff leather couch and wait, eyes examining the faded beige of the office walls.

A few minutes later, a girl I don't recognize opens the door and walks up to Mrs. Ortiz. "Hello, my name is Elizabeth Richards," she says with a genuine, could-melt-the-ice-caps smile.

"Hello, Ms. Richards. Yes, we've been waiting for you. Welcome!" Mrs. Ortiz stands from her seat and walks around her desk to embrace the new girl, who first hesitates, but then returns the gesture. "We have your transfer papers all ready to go."

"Great!" I study the new girl – transfer student, apparently – from my seat. Her honey-colored hair falls in waves, brushing past her shoulders. She wears a yellow sweater with *look at the stars* printed on the back and denim jeans that are just tight enough with holes in the knees. Mom always told me leering at a woman wasn't right, so I look away because just now I hear her voice inside my head, somehow managing to mother me when she's not even in the same city.

Mrs. Ortiz smiles – perhaps too enthusiastically. "Your admissions officer will be right with you. Please feel free to take a seat."

"Thank you very much," Elizabeth says as she turns.

Her blue eyes meet mine for a second.

Please don't sit next to me... I tell myself because I'm not in the mood for social interaction. Of course, I'm never in the mood so I guess I'm just anti-social.

Ignorant of my inner plea, she walks right up to me and extends a hand. "Hi. I'm Elizabeth."

I smile back and wonder if mine is as genuine and warm as hers or it's sterile and cold like the receptionist's. "Hi. I'm Adam."

"It's nice to meet you, Adam," she says, sitting in the seat next to mine.

I lean forward, elbows on my knees, locking my fingers together. My jaw tenses and I hope that I can just wait out the silence. But I have a thing about first impressions. I don't want to leave room for assumptions. So I feel somehow obligated to fill the silence, to maintain a normal conversation with the new girl, to make her feel welcome. To be normal and friendly. So I ask, "Where did you transfer from?"

"I was going to a community college in LA. I wanted the full college experience so I decided to come here."

"Mm-hmm. So you moved from the City of Angels to San Francisco?" I laugh. "There's nothing but devils here, I'm afraid."

She smiles, her hands folded neatly in her lap. "I guess you could say I needed a change of scenery," she replies with a wink. "Besides, I've never seen the Golden Gate Bridge before. Thought it'd be fun. *New*."

"So have you?" She cocks an eyebrow at me. "Seen the

Golden Gate Bridge, I mean. Have you gone to see it yet?"

In an instant, I'm brought back to the bridge before sunrise this morning and I recall with vivid precision the cold iron bridge. "Up close and personal," I say. The eyes are the windows to the soul and I wonder if she sees through mine.

"Ms. Richards?"

Her head turns toward the voice at the end of the hallway. "Yes?"

"My name is Claire Bennet and I'll be your admissions officer."

Elizabeth stands up to shake the woman's hand. "It's great to finally meet you in person," she laughs.

The sound takes me by surprise. It's bright and deep. It isn't fake.

"And you as well. We're so excited that you've decided to come be a part of our community."

Community. I stifle a laugh.

"If you could follow me this way?" Claire says, turning toward the hallway.

"Of course." Elizabeth starts after her, but turns back before she rounds the corner. "It was nice to meet you, Adam."

"You too, Elizabeth."

She smiles and vanishes behind the wall just as Doctor Keller comes out. "Good afternoon, Adam. Ready for our session?"

"Would I be here if I wasn't?"

He smirks and I know he's already judging me, assessing

my mental state. "If you'll please follow me." He says the same thing every time, as if he thinks I haven't figured out where his office is by now.

We step inside the small office and I sit down on the other side of him. Leaning back, I cross my arms, eyes focused on the surface of the desk. My mind wanders to the bridge this morning and my chest tightens as I remember the feeling when I slipped and almost fell. With a sharp inhale, my mind then flashes to Elizabeth Richards and her smile. I can't get away from it. It was the kind of smile that said, "I see you."

Dr. Keller pulls a yellow notepad and pen out of a drawer and sets it in front of him, straightening it so that it lines up perfectly with the big calendar on his desk. In red, I see my name circled in one of the boxes.

"How are you doing, Adam?"

"Fine," I say.

I catch him eying my sleeves. I put my hands under the edge of the desk.

"Let me see your wrists, Adam."

With a smirk, I hold my breath and slip my sleeve up just far enough for him to see the scars. What he can't see is the fresh scars on my chest and shoulders. But he doesn't need to know that. I never wanted people to see the scars. The rumors would fly quickly. Especially here. But no one notices them anyway. *No one wants to.*

Keller scrawls an obscure note on his yellow pad with surgical precision. I try to read it upside down, but fail. I fall back in my seat with a grunt as I roll my sleeves back down.

My mind flashes to my first day of fourth grade eight-and-a-half years ago. I remember the song those mean little kids made up, turning my last name into a joke. "West is the worst," they would sing. "West is the worst." Over and over, they taunted me. As if I wasn't a person. Eventually, I learned to ignore it, tune it out.

Eventually I grew numb to it.

"How are things at home?" His glasses are perched low on his nose. I wonder if he does that on purpose just so he can stare down at me with those narrow eyes.

I shrug. "It's good. My mom works a lot. She's tired all the time. I wish I could help her somehow..." I pause, clear my throat. "She doesn't know anything about any of this. But she loves me." I don't blame my mom for not understanding or even knowing. I love her. She's all I have. I'm all she has. I just wish I was better for her. I wish I could make her feel safe again. I wish I could be there for her the way she needs. If there's one thing I know for certain it's that my issues are the last thing she needs to worry about.

In the last eight months I've been officially and unofficially diagnosed with Bipolar Disorder (Officially), Borderline Personality Disorder (Officially), and Post Traumatic Stress Disorder (Unofficially. I diagnosed myself with that one. Thanks, Google.)

"Any suicidal thoughts lately?"

"No." *Always.*

"Have you been praying?"

"Are you really asking me that?" I scoff.

He frowns. "You can't let what you're going through

defeat you, Adam. Face your goliath."

I can't withhold the laugh as it bursts from my chest. "I'm *already* defeated, Doc. Your advice is too little, too late. I'm a walking dead man."

"No one is beyond redemption. No one is beyond victory. You need to reconnect with God. Maybe separate yourself from some things that are detrimental to your mental, emotional, and spiritual health."

"You don't get it, do you?" I lean into my hands. "I don't even know if I believe there is a God anymore." I'm resigned to it, I think. But I guess if God ever did show up then maybe things could change. But for now, it's just me – Adam West against the world. "And even if God *is* real, I don't think He wants anything to do with me."

"It sounds to me like you've given up, Adam. God's always there for you. He's always for you. You've got to learn how to look past everything that's happening inside of you and start seeing things from a new perspective. Reconnect with Him and it will change the way you see things. It may not change your circumstances, but it could change who you are in the middle of your circumstance. Maybe everything you've gone through is only a chapter in the story God wants to write. It's all shaping you into the man you're going to become."

Scoffing inwardly, I glide my fingers across my lips. "Yeah, well..." Part of me knows that he's probably right. And part of me doesn't care.

His gaze softens and I feel bad for a second because I know he's doing what he can to help; it's just that, at this point, I'm beyond help.

"Have you thought more about taking medication?"

I grind my teeth. The question takes my mind back to months prior. The memories are faded now, but I remember sitting in a Starbucks with *him.*

I finger the sleeve of my mocha and watch the steam rise through the mouth of the lid, chewing at the inside of my lips. I take a sip as Jeremiah sits down across from me.

"How's the mocha?"

"It's good," I nod.

He smiles at me so I offer a half-hearted smile in response. "Thanks for paying."

Nodding, he takes a sip of his own drink. "How's your studying for mid-terms coming along?"

"I haven't even started," I laugh.

"Dude, there's only a week left! Better get on it, like, as soon as we get back to campus."

"Yeah."

"Hey. Are you okay?" he asks after a minute. I feel bad for how awkward it is for him whenever I get bad. I mentally kick myself for being such a burden, but secretly I'm grateful for the attention. Selfish, I know, but it feels... nice to have someone invest some of their time in you, to spend time getting to know the real you, to understand all your secrets. Someone who cares enough to push through the walls.

If only I could push through them myself.

"I'm fine. Just tired," I say.

"*Right,*" he says sarcastically. "*I've known you long enough now to know when that's true and when it isn't. So don't pull that with me, okay?*"

I look up at him. He stares at me, his brow furrowed in genuine concern. He scratches at his beard and reaches to readjust his beanie. A lock of blonde hair falls in front of his eyes. I stare at him for a second, wondering what I did to deserve a friend like him. He's been beside me through more in the past five months than anyone has my entire life.

I smile. "*Okay,*" I say. "*I guess I'm just... having a low day.*"

He nods. "*Have you talked with Dr. Keller about taking any medication?*"

"*He's mentioned it, but I'm not really sure how I feel about it.*" I pause. "*I mean, if I get an official diagnosis and they prescribe some meds, then it suddenly becomes real. I can't pretend it isn't there anymore. But at the same time... an official diagnosis would confirm that there is actually something wrong with me and it's not just all in my head.*" I wince inwardly, my stomach tightens.

"*Look, Adam, you just have to treat mental illness like any other disease. It's no different than cancer or the flu. It's a disease that needs to be treated. And acting like it doesn't exist is not healthy – for you or anyone who cares about you.*"

"*Yeah...*" I say.

He leans back in his chair. "*How does your mom feel about all this? Have you even told her any of the stuff you've told me?*"

I shake my head. "I can't tell her. She doesn't need that in her life. She's been through enough."

"You've gotta stop thinking like that, man."

I shrug. "I can't help it." I take a drink of my mocha, savoring the warmth it provides against the backdrop of San Francisco's autumn rain. I catch Jeremiah looking at me and hold his gaze for a brief second.

"We should head back to campus," I say.

He nods as we both stand and shove our chairs in. "Time to hit the books."

We head to his car, a green Toyota, and before we get in, Jeremiah grabs me by the shoulder and pulls me into a hug. Taken by surprise, my arms hang limp at my sides for a minute before I return the gesture.

"You know I've always got your back, Adam. You're like the little brother I never had."

My eyes burn and I blink back tears. An only child with no real friends, I've never had anyone to talk to. Jeremiah was the first person to really see me.

"Don't ever let go, okay? Don't ever give up. I'm not sick of you and God's not sick of you." He pulls back and stares at me. "I know I'm not perfect, but I'm here for you."

"Thank you," I say, clearing my throat. "That means a lot." And it really does.

He smiles again. "You're welcome." He ruffles my hair, breaking the solemnity and says, "Now let's go study!"

I hop in his car and buckle up as he pulls out of the Starbucks parking lot.

In an instant, I'm brought back to the sterile smell of Doctor Keller's office as he repeats my name. "Adam?"

I shake the memory from my head. "Huh?" I shift in my seat. "I'm sorry, could you repeat the question?"

"Have you thought anymore about taking medication?" he asks as he scribbles another note.

I quell the urge to throw that stupid, yellow notepad across the room.

"I don't know. I'm open to it, I guess." If I owed Jeremiah for anything, it's for helping me treat mental illness like a disease and not a character flaw.

"Well, keep thinking on it and let me know when you've decided. Don't be so quick to dismiss something that could potentially help you in the long run."

I nod.

The numbness starts to wrap itself around my body again, like an icy stiffness that spreads from my chest to the rest of my body. It traps me inside my mind with the shadows I've tried so long to forget.

I don't hear Dr. Keller as he starts talking to me about my mom and God and school, saying the same things he always says. I just sit there, unmoving, biting at the raw flesh on the inside of my lips.

I guess if I could say that I felt anything in this moment, it might be contempt. Contempt for myself. Contempt for Jeremiah. Contempt for the people around me - the people who pretend they don't see me.

And that contempt never leaves me alone. It's ruthless. Merciless. And it pulls me deeper and deeper into the shadows, ensuring that no one will *ever* see me. *Please. Someone. See me.*

4

Tuesday morning brings the memory of a gentle smile to the forefront of my weary mind. As I lie here, the morning light filtering through my dorm room window, my mind is a mirage of fragmented memories and dreams. They're distorted fractals of countless stories that I've stored inside. It's both a blessing and a curse to be greeted each morning by the memories of days gone by.

Today could be different.

Sitting upright in bed, I grab my journal and fold it open in my lap. I stare at the empty lines full of infinite possibility, a future waiting to be claimed. A story waiting to be told.

Today is a new day, I write. I don't know if it's hope I feel, or that strange euphoric feeling that comes with a bipolar "high", but I write it down anyway. Because every bright moment needs to be remembered like landmarks through the miles of madness.

My heart seems to put itself on pause as Elizabeth comes to mind. I see her eyes as clearly as if she were right in front of me. The mere memory of that look in her eyes is like a siren song, spurring me into maddening curiosity.

I met a girl yesterday. She smiled at me. I think I need to know her, I write, the tip of my pen tearing into the page of my journal, the ink spilling onto the page. *I can't explain it, but today could be different and tomorrow might be better and I think I need to know her.*

Flipping through the pages of my journal, I find a folded piece of familiar yellow paper. I let it dangle between my fingers a minute before I begin to unfold it with care. Studying it, remembering every word, retracing the path the pen took, losing myself in the drops of blood that stain the page.

Folding the piece of paper up and setting it aside, I pick up my pen and write again.

I will make tomorrow better. I will know her. She will be my one last adventure. What have I got to lose?

I close my journal, grab my towel, and head to the showers.

I see her in my first class of the day, *Intro to Philosophy.* I sit in the far back row in the far right corner and she sits one row up, but on the far left. I count the spaces and seats between us. Two tables, thirteen chairs, thirteen strangers whose names I don't recall.

My laptop is open in front of me, my fingers lingering on the keys, interrupted mid-sentence. Out of the corner of my eye, I watch her, her attention fixed on our professor.

By the time my mind returns to the lecture, the conversation has become a debate about heaven and hell and what different religious organizations believe about them.

"There are some who believe Hell is simply the end of our individual existence," Professor Garcia says. "They take the atheistic idea that after death, we simply cease all being, and meld it together with this idea of Hell. So in the end, we have the righteous, who spend eternity in Heaven, and the unrighteous who simply cease to exist. This is called Annihilationism.

"Then, there are those who believe that the absolute end of existence is incentive enough for someone to believe in their respective deities and that there needn't be more."

A few rows over, Jeremiah raises his hand. "Doesn't the book of Revelation talk about what hell is like? Doesn't it mention the *lake of fire*?"

Garcia smiles, nods, and says, "Many scholars believe that due to the apocalyptic nature of the book of Revelation, the descriptions of the Apostle John's visions are intentionally far-fetched in order to convey surrealist ideals. Much like J.R.R. Tolkien's *Lord of the Rings* saga, the book of Revelation was a fantastical story to give the believer an idea of what the 'end' might look like. It was John's way of utilizing the human imagination to get his point across.

"Mind you, I'm not here to tell you what to believe. I simply wish to enable you to make an informed decision. It's up to each of you as individuals and free-thinkers to apply these things to your own lives." He pauses. "Would anyone else like to share their thoughts of Heaven and Hell?"

Nobody raises their hand at first. Until I raise mine.

I'm not entirely sure what came over me, but here I am. No going back now.

"Go ahead, Mr. West."

Clearing my throat, I swallow. I glance to where

Elizabeth Richards sits and our eyes meet briefly. Is she ever not smiling?

I return my attention to the professor. "I believe that hell is something we see every day." I pause. "Every time we see suffering and pain, we see a fragment of what Hell is like. When you walk past the homeless man, the addict. When you hear stories about murder, rape, assault, or robbery. When you see the orphan, the widow, the lost, the poor. Those are *mere fragments* of what Hell is like.

"Take those times when you feel most alone, most scared, most lost, most hopeless, most worthless, most abandoned, most hurt, most broken, most separated from God... and multiply it by infinity. That is hell." Finished now, my heart beats so fast that I'm not sure it'll ever slow down. Jaw tense, I inhale sharply through my nose and hope nobody notices the tension that I'm positive is written all over my face.

"Thank you, Mr. West. That is a very... *provocative* perspective." His eyes flicker to the other side of the room. "Go ahead, Ms. Richards."

"Adding onto what Adam said, we can apply the same perspective to Heaven. While, yes, we see fragments of Hell seeping in through the fractures of a broken world, we can also see fragments of Heaven breaking in. When a stranger buys that homeless man a meal. When people from all backgrounds and faiths join together to provide relief to those who suffered from natural disasters. When a mother holds her baby for the first time. When the sun sets at the end of a perfect day. These are the moments when Heaven shines through in the midst of Hell on earth."

She looks right at me and says, "Yeah. Hell is real. But I think heaven is the greater reality. Most people just don't look for it."

It's hard for me to believe that someone could have such a positive view of the world. I don't understand it. But there's something about it - something about the way she talks about heaven - there's a goodness there. A kindness in her voice. It pierces me. And I think that in that moment, as her eyes catch mine, heaven becomes real again.

I manage to catch her as we leave class. "Elizabeth Richards," I say. "That was quite the speech. And on your first day in class, no less. Impressive."

Clutching her books to her chest with both hands, she laughs the kind of laugh I would expect. "Oh? And yours wasn't too bad either. The world needs people who aren't blind to darkness."

If only she knew. "I think it would take a pretty ignorant person not to see the darkness in the world. But..." I smile. "It takes someone special to see the light."

We both pause for a minute and stare at each other.

Crossing my arms, I smile. "How about I take you on a tour of the city tonight? It wouldn't be right to welcome you to the Bay any other way."

She smiles. "I'd like that."

I release an inner sigh of relief. "Great! Meet me outside the dorms at 7 tonight." I start to leave, then add, "You're not afraid of heights, are you?"

She cocks an eyebrow. "No. Why?"

I smile. "Just curious." Then I leave.

My second class is over. *Applied Mathematics.* (I *really* hate math.)

I beeline for the men's dorms through the throng of students. Just as I pull the door open, he rounds the corner and slams into me. We both drop our books and papers everywhere.

"Sorry," I mutter as I stoop to gather my mess. I look up to see Jeremiah frowning back at me as he retrieves his own books. I feel him staring and divert my attention back to my books.

He stands and walks past me without a word.

Clutching the scattered pages in my arms, I can feel it in my chest, swelling, rising, boiling in my veins. *Breathe*, I remind myself. *Inhale. Exhale.* I stand there, breathing, waiting until my body is once again under my control before I lock myself in my dorm room.

The silence is welcome. Without a roommate, I have the fortune of solitude.

Opening my pantry, I stare at my reflection in the mirror on the back of the door. I think of all the things I am and all the things I'm not as the pain begins to spread its icy fingers over every inch of my flesh.

Watching my eyes in the mirror, they begin to burn and my vision blurs, but the tears don't fall. Not today. I will not be weak.

With a cry, I release the pain and my fist shatters the

man in the mirror.

Standing outside the women's dorm hours later, I find myself nervous. What am I doing? I just met this girl. This is unusual, even for me. Even on my *good* days. I pace the sidewalk, waiting for her, fingering the bandage on my knuckles.

The door opens and she walks out just as the clock on my phone switches to 7:03. I smile as she wanders toward me, smiling back. Watching her closely, my eyes make note of every single detail. This time, she wears a fuzzy, grey sweater that sort of drapes over her slender frame, so low that it almost reaches her knees. She pulls a grey beanie down over her hair. Next to her, I feel mildly underdressed in my black jeans, black tee, flannel button-down, and backwards cap.

I stand there for a moment until I realize I'm staring and it's starting to get weird. "Ready for a night on the town?"

"Absolutely."

I arch my spine, thrusting my shoulders back and clicking my heels together, holding my elbow out to her.

She raises an eyebrow. "Mr. West," she says, "chivalry isn't dead after all."

I lead her to where Gus is parked and hold the passenger side door open for her. "Elizabeth Richards, meet *Gus the Bus.* He's quite temperamental, but a loyal sidekick through all my exploits."

She runs her hand along the door frame, inspecting the vehicle. "Hi, Gus. I'm Liz. It's a pleasure to meet you."

With a smile, I close the door behind her and round the bus to the driver's side, sliding behind the steering wheel.

I turn the key, but the engine doesn't start. I glance over to Elizabeth who just watches, amused. "Like I said... *temperamental.*" I punch the dash and Gus roars to life.

"Right. Of course." She nods, smothering a laugh.

Shifting the van into reverse, I pull out of the parking space. I circle the lot and come to the gate, stopping a moment before merging with traffic.

For a while we drive in silence. Glancing as often as I can, I see her staring out the window, watching the city as it passes in a blur of graffiti, concrete, and light. Excitement bubbles in her eyes as she absorbs the passing San Francisco cityscape. Suburbia fades into the distance and the fast-paced flicker of downtown rises to meet us as we merge with the heartbeat of the city. The sunset dances on glass buildings that press into its light.

In the passenger seat, I see her picking at her fingernails. She's nervous. I don't blame her. I am too. The inside of my lip is raw from biting it. How do you get to know people? I don't think I remember what that looks like. What kind of things do people talk about?

When the sun begins to disappear behind the city, I ask, "You hungry?"

"Yeah."

"I know a place."

"I'm sure you do." From the corner of my eyes, I see her smiling at me. "You seem like a guy who gets around."

"If I stay standing in one place for too long the world might leave me behind." I smile over at her, but she kind of just pauses, stares at me, lips parted, but she doesn't say anything.

It's called *The Plank*, a restaurant nestled among the skyscrapers along the bay. Outside, there's a nice courtyard between the restaurant and the bay that joins with other bars and businesses. The waiter leads us to our booth after a few minutes and we sit down across from each other.

"So, tell me about yourself." She straightens her coaster underneath her glass, so that it is perfectly parallel to the edge of the table. "Who *is* Elizabeth Richards?"

"Well," she clears her throat, "first, you can call me Liz. Anytime someone calls me by my full name I automatically assume I'm in trouble." She laughs and so do I.

"Okay, Liz. Tell me about yourself."

"Alright, well, I'm nineteen and I'm majoring in Secondary Education. I'm originally from Seattle, Washington before my parents moved our family to LA. Oh, and I'm an only child." She takes a sip of her water.

"No, I mean, *who are you?* Here." I point to my heart. "What makes you tick? I don't want trivia, I want soul, y'know? C'mon, give me some soul."

A faint blush brightens her complexion as she stares across at me, hesitant. I don't blame her. It took me a long time to open up to someone about those kinds of things. So I guess that's why I ask. Because I know how important it was for me when I found that for myself. And there's a part of me that, when I look at someone, I want to make sure that I'm never the reason that they don't feel like they can be real. Raw. Honest. Maybe that comes from knowing that I've lost that. Maybe it's more for me than it is for her, because if she can show me her deepest places, then maybe I could show her mine.

"Please?" I ask with a bit of a laugh. Maybe it's for both of us.

Sighing, "You sure do ask the easy questions don't you."

I chuckle. "There are no easy questions." Shrugging, I add, "At least, not that I've found."

"Hmm... Fair enough." She lifts her fingers and fidgets with the hem of her beanie, brushing a loose lock of hair behind her ear. "I don't know, I guess. I mean, I *know*, but..." She squints at me, shifting in her seat. "How do you put something like that into words, y'know? How do you describe the truest parts of your being when our vocabulary isn't big enough? When there aren't enough words to describe the thoughts and hopes and dreams and fears that make you who you are? It's impossible to articulate the human spirit because it's just too big."

In the pause, I smile and stare right at her. I will make sure she knows that I see her. "Elizabeth Richards, you are a veritable sea."

She laughs. "If you say so."

I smile at her. She smiles back just as the waitress comes to take our order. "I'll have a bacon cheeseburger with fries, please."

"And you, miss?"

"Uh," she glances at the menu. "I'll have a Caesar salad,

please."

"And to drink?"

"Just some lemon for my water," I say, my eyes fixed on the girl across from me.

"Same," she says."

"Alright, your lemon will be right out." The waitress takes our menus and turns to leave.

"Thank you," I say. Out of the corner of my eye, I notice her just watching me quietly.

"So why are you doing this, Adam?" she asks.

"Doing what?"

"Taking me out to dinner, to see the city. I'm sure you have better things to do than to show the new girl a good time."

I stare at her for a second, trying to figure out how to answer that – trying to decide if I even know the answer. Finally, I say, "Because I know what it's like to feel alone in a room full of strangers. And knowing that makes it my responsibility to do whatever it takes to make sure no one else ever has to feel that way."

She stares at me, a sparkle in her eyes. She's all smiles. "That's very sweet. Thank you."

"You're welcome." The waitress returns with our lemon and I immediately squeeze it into my water, taking a sip, my throat suddenly dry.

"So what about you? What's your story?" she asks, leaning forward.

I stare at my glass, my fingers wiping at the condensation, my eyes tracing each trail. Lifting my eyes, I look back at her and let my smile hang between us and just then I realize that I don't think I've really stopped smiling all evening. "My story belongs to the ocean."

She raises an eyebrow.

I lean forward to meet her and whisper, looking out of the corner of my eyes in both directions, as if prepared to share a secret with her. "I hope depths don't frighten you."

"Not at all. I love a good adventure," she says, a glimmer of maybe both mischief and intrigue in her eye.

"Perfect."

When we finish eating, I call for the check.

"Why the rush?" she asks as I give the waitress two twenty dollar bills and tell her to keep the change.

"There's something I want to show you."

We leave the restaurant behind for city streets bathed in twilight. My hands fixed on the steering wheel, I glance at her as she stares out the window, her eyes following every dark alley and sidewalk. She grabs the crank and turns it, lowering the window. She lifts herself up from her seat and climbs out to sit on the window frame. As if to claim a victory, she raises her arms to catch the wind, shouting into the icy air. In response, the wind almost carries her beanie away, but she grabs it just in time and takes it off so that her hair billows behind her like the tail of a comet.

The city is behind us now. I can feel the transition as we move from smooth city streets to bumpy country roads. It seems as though it's been hours by the time I pull over. Parking at the side of the road, I remove the keys and hop out.

"Where are we?" she asks.

"You'll see," I say as I climb the hillside. Over the knoll there's an old water tower, the last remnant of a long-abandoned ranch. One of the things I love about the San Francisco Bay Area is that farms, ranches, and vineyards fill the hills between cities. It's a perfect balance of city life and country life and the smell of fertilizer in the air is just strong enough to make you feel like you live in simpler times.

She summits the hill behind me just as I start to walk down and she follows me all the way to the water tower. I grab hold of the wooden rungs and start to climb, ignoring their protests. "Follow me."

When we reach the top, I lie down on old wood boards, careful to avoid any loose nails, and stare up at the night sky. The cityscape glimmers in the distance, but doesn't completely diminish the stars above us.

She lies down beside me, our arms touching just enough that I feel her warmth.

"I come here a lot," I tell her. "This is one of my favorite places. Out in the middle of nowhere, touched by time and forgotten by humanity. I like it here because when I look up at the stars in the middle of the night it reminds me that there are things out there that are so much bigger than whatever is right here, right now. Sometimes, I'll try to count the stars just to put a number on them. I don't know why, but it helps give me some peace when everything in my life seems... out of balance."

"Wow," she whispers. "I thought stars were cool before,

but now..."

I laugh. "I know what you mean. Sometimes, you look at extraordinary stuff for so long, it starts to become ordinary. Sometimes you have to take back your wonder from whoever stole it form you."

"And has anyone ever stolen yours from you?" she asks. It's almost as if a part of her knows. Just like a part of me knows that there's something different about her. It's not like I know any specifics. But there's a sort of knowing inside of me that comes when you meet someone who's been through deep, rough places like you have. There's an age in eyes that have seen dark places. And there's a wonder in eyes that still see the light in the middle of all of that.

"Yeah. There have been a few people and situations." It goes deeper than that, but I'm not sure I'm ready to tell her. I'm not sure she's ready to know. "What about you?"

She shifts beside me. "Yeah. A few. I think that's just life, though."

"Life is a cruel master," I laugh.

"Maybe. Sometimes. But... life can be beautiful too."

I think on that for a minute. What does a beautiful life look like? The first thought in my mind is that it looks like the wonder in her eyes. "Tell me what you see, Liz." What is it like to see through eyes of wonder? A part of me needs to know because it's as if she carries something I haven't felt in a long time.

"No one's ever asked me anything like that before," she muses, her voice a whisper so fragile it might be broken by the breeze.

"I guess I'm *no one*." My lips smile, but even though they're my own, the words sting.

She sighs. "The lies we tell ourselves..." Pausing, I feel her thinking beside me. "I see a universe full of endless light."

This time, every part of me smiles. "That's what I like about you, Liz," I say, my eyes gazing intently at the stars. "You're an optimist. You're the only girl I've ever met who sees the light in an ocean of black."

There is silence between us, but it's not awkward. It's comfortable. It's right. It's *real.*

"There's enough darkness in this world," she says. "It's easy to see darkness. It takes real effort to see light." She says that in a way that tells me she's been there. And I admire that about her; that she's been in the black, but can still see the light.

And we lay here, completely still and silent, watching the stars end and begin. The moments pass slowly until, all of the sudden, Liz's fingertips brush against mine and time stands still.

And in the middle of all this black, I think I'm finally starting to see the stars.

5

Most people begin their mornings with a nice cup of coffee. I begin mine with a cigarette.

Standing on the dormitory roof, I watch the sun rise above the city. I flick the ash from the cigarette and return it to its place at my lips. I inhale, the smoke flooding my lungs, seeping into the fibers of my existence. I close my eyes and for a second I feel Liz's fingertips brush against mine again, sending my mind back to that night just a week ago. We didn't get back to the campus until sometime after midnight so we had to sneak into the dorms without waking up our Resident Advisors. If they caught us, we'd receive a warning. Well, she would. My punishment might have been a little more severe since it wasn't exactly my first offense.

After watching the stars from the top of the water tower, we spent the rest of the time (I don't know how long) driving across the countryside, admiring the vineyards and their million-dollar mansions.

We didn't talk much, but we were there. Together. Under the stars. And it felt good, to be with someone, to feel her beside me, to hear every breath she took. It felt good to know that in that moment if I disappeared, she, at least, would notice.

We haven't seen much of each other since that night, though we text constantly. I imagine she's probably been studying and I, as always, have been off doing my own thing. I see her in class, though, and she always acknowledges me with a smile, which is nice. And I always smile back. I'd forgotten what it feels like to be noticed by someone, to look up and see someone glance over at you with kindness in their eyes.

Slipping my journal from my backpack, I sit cross-legged on the roof and begin to write.

Everyone matters. You'll never meet anyone who doesn't matter. Even the bad people. And maybe people come and go in your life, but they all matter. They matter because with everything they say and do and feel, they make you. This dance of spirit and flesh, of soul and bone, it matters. It affects everything and everyone around you.

Because it matters.

As the sun and moon move, breathing life into the waves, so moves every beating heart. You can't explain the harmony of it all, life and love, joy and sadness, anger and madness, but it's all there, working together like the sun and the moon as they create the waves and the tide.

Pausing, I let the words at my fingertips take root in the caverns of my being. I stare at nothing in particular for a long while, lost in time, lost in thought, until I return to the pages that hold it all together in front of me.

Maybe my heart is the moon and hers is the sun and everything else is gravity.

Taking one last drag, I close my journal, shove it in my backpack, and stand to my feet. Dropping the last of the cigarette on the roof, I grind it into the concrete with my heel, pop a piece of peppermint gum into my mouth, and climb down the ladder on the backside of the building.

I make my way to the auditorium for Wednesday morning announcements. I'm the last one in so I sit in the back row as the Dean makes his way to the podium. It isn't a big auditorium; it only fits roughly a hundred people. Even still, it's easy to get lost in the crowd when the entire student body is together in the same room. I'm thankful for that because I feel safe and secure, hidden from notice by dozens of bodies and my denim jacket.

"Good morning, students," the Dean says.

Scattered murmurs of reply float from the crowd.

Just as I'm scanning the crowd in search of Liz, my phone vibrates in my pocket and I pull it out to see a text from her.

LIZ
You owe me a tour of the rest of the city. We never did see the Golden Gate Bridge.

I guess we got sidetracked. I text back.

ME
Liz, I'm gonna show you the world.

LIZ
Quite the over-achiever, aren't you?

ME
Life is short. Why settle?

LIZ
"You've only got so long to live." Sylvia Plath

She doesn't know the half of it.

ME

Be still, my heart. She reads poetry.

LIZ

The finer things in life, right?

ME

AND she's a girl after my own heart.

LIZ

Hahaha

I return my attention to the announcements just in time to hear the Dean mention my name. "We have a small group of prospective students with us today. The administration has selected three currently enrolled students to accompany them to a private luncheon. Those students are Adam West, Jeremiah Jackson, and Oliver Lopez. Please meet with Professor Garcia in front of the Admin Building after your first class. You've received excused absences for the classes you will be missing."

I freeze. My stomach twists inside me and my heart stops beating as soon as I hear the other two names announced. I can't breathe.

Nononono

My fingers dig into the arm of my chair and I feel like I might throw up. I resist the urge, clamping my jaw tight.

If there's a God, He has a cruel sense of humor.

Dread seeps into my nerves, infecting every shadowed

part of my existence. Memories brutally assault my sense and it's all I can do not to run from the auditorium and find a trash can to dispose of the anxiety that's currently laying waste to my mind.

A thousand thoughts flash across my mind, but the only thing I can think is, *I can't do this. I can't do this.* And I repeat it in my head over and over and over.

Glad now that I sat in the back row, I sneak out to find the restroom just in time to vomit a brutal concoction of last night's dinner and maybe a small amount of cigarette ash into the toilet. My hands grasp the toilet seat as I sit on the floor of the bathroom, a series of unwelcome tremors racing across my bones.

Breathe, I remind myself. *In, out, in, out, in, out, in.*

I've been here before. On this floor, shaking. Angry. Sick. Unable to think about anything except how broken everything has become. Leaning against the wall of the restroom stall, I look up at the flickering fluorescent light and try to remember what it felt like that night a week ago to look up at the stars and catch a glimpse of wonder. At the time, I'd thought maybe things would change. Maybe it would start to get better. Maybe opening up to someone new could help me escape the hurt inside of me. But none of that could ever get rid of the endless sea of black that hides behind it all. It doesn't just go away. When the hurt buries itself inside of you, it touches everything. Every word, every thought, every desire, every dream. The shadows hide behind it all.

And I'm not sure there will ever be an escape. Maybe I

don't want there to be.

My heart stops racing and I finally get my feet under me. I flush the toilet and turn to leave, but my eye catches the graffiti on the stall door. My graffiti. *I exist,* in bold, black letters. Except sometime in the last week, someone scratched a line through it. Seeing it, my heart sinks. Knowing that someone could simply put a line through my existence... that someone could censor my life... it breaks something inside of me. It rips open every old wound and I don't know that I have the strength to recover.

Unlocking the stall door, I step out and almost bump into Oliver. He doesn't acknowledge my presence so I return the favor and leave the restroom.

I need a smoke.

I spent my first class period smoking (pot this time; if I have to go to lunch with Jeremiah and Oliver, I'm going stoned out of my mind) on the dorm roof again. It's a nasty habit. I really should quit. Inwardly, I laugh at the notion as I make my way, now, to the front of the Admin Building.

Professor Garcia, Jeremiah, and Oliver wait for me. Garcia speaks before anyone else has a chance (and in my head I thank him for it). "The prospective students are waiting for us at the Canterbury Dining Hall. We'll carpool there. And don't worry, your meals will be covered by the school," he says.

Jeremiah and Oliver nod, but I just stand there, my mind drifting as the cannabis begins to take its hold on my system. My muscles begin to relax as Garcia leads the way to one of the school vans. Oliver follows right behind Garcia, talking to him about something that I don't really care about. I'm lagging behind when Jeremiah turns around suddenly to face me and I startle, stepping back. I try my best to keep my face expressionless. I will not be weak. Never again.

"Are you stoned?" he whispers, his face tense, lips drawn tight.

I say nothing and he scoffs.

"Grow up," he says, shaking his head and walking away.

I stay behind a minute, resisting the urge to ditch the luncheon altogether. But I know I can't. Garcia would tell the Dean and then the Dean would tell my counselor. And frankly, I don't feel like giving my counselor any more ammunition to shrink me with. I shrink myself enough as it is.

So I take a deep breath, my eyes burning, and walk to the van. I climb in the back seat and stick my earbuds in. Clicking on the Pandora app, I select my Indie Rock station, letting the music transport me somewhere far, far, *far* away.

The Canterbury is abuzz with the sound of conversations that I spend most of the time trying to avoid. Unfortunately, most people are fairly clueless when someone's intentionally trying to be antisocial.

"How do you like the school?" one of the prospective students – a brunette with a round face and deep, green eyes – asks, leaning forward as if her very existence depends on my answer.

I admire her eyes as I answer, "The food is great and the classes are worth it." I glance at Jeremiah who sits with Oliver a few chairs away. "The people, not so much. Most of them, anyway."

Unsure how to respond, her lips slightly parted but silent, she leans back. "Oh." Clearing her throat, she turns away.

Mission: be as antisocial as possible. Status: accomplished. Honestly, I'm doing her a favor. Saving her from a world of hurt. Even if she doesn't know it.

I watch Jeremiah now, talking and laughing and having a good time with Oliver and the prospective students. And then our eyes meet for a second, but I don't look away. I stare right at him, daring him to say something, do something, to finish what he started, letting my eyes tell him all the things he never let me say. My jaw is tense as my teeth combat each other. My heart aches and my stomach swallows itself. But I don't look away, not for one second. *I* never look away. *I* shouldn't have to.

So I stare directly at him, watching him grow uneasy with every second our eyes stay connected. And then he looks away. But I still don't. Because I'm not in the Canterbury anymore. I'm somewhere else. I'm someone else, someone who doesn't exist anymore.

In the restrooms of the men's dorm, I see Jeremiah and Oliver standing at the urinals as I step into the stall closest to the door.

"Dude, I just don't think I can do this anymore," Jeremiah says.

I pause.

"What do you mean?" Oliver asks, flushing.

"Adam. It's the same thing over and over again. I don't know what else to do. Honestly, it's like he likes being depressed. It doesn't seem like anything I say or do does anything to help. And whenever he walks into the room it's like this dark cloud follows him and it just totally takes over everything. I don't feel like I can relax because I'm constantly worried about saying the wrong thing. And I feel like I spend so much of my time trying to help him that I don't even have a life of my own anymore. I'm sick of it. I can't do it anymore."

Frozen, my mouth hangs open and a lump begins to form in my throat as my mind attempts to process what I'd just heard. My heart turns to lead and I'm falling through the floor, the last of me disappearing out of sight. I blink back tears as I realize that one of my closest friends was not only talking down about me, but he was doing it behind my back. My heart collapses in on itself until all that's left is a giant black hole where my heart used to be.

I have to get out of there. I try to unlock the stall door quietly, but my nerves get the best of me and the door slams into the side of the stall before I can catch it.

Jeremiah and Oliver stand at the sink and Jeremiah's eyes widen when he sees me in the reflection of the mirror.

"Adam, I-" he stammers.

I don't stay for an explanation and, swinging the

restroom door open, I storm out. I hear Jeremiah chasing me, but I don't turn around.

My face is confused, I think. My eyes burn with anger and my chest aches with grief. The walls of my mind, lined with every broken thing I ever thought about myself, cave in on me. It's all in pieces laid out in front of me and I race to put it all back together, but I don't think that's possible anymore.

"Adam, wait!" I don't. "Wait!" he shouts again.

Stopping, I spin to face him, teeth clenched. "What do you want?"

"Adam, I'm sorry," he starts.

"For what?" I can feel the tears winning the battle and I hate that I look so weak in front of him, but I feel everything within me crumble and fall apart and I can't help it. "For not believing in me? For being - how did you put it? - sick and tired of me? What are you sorry for? For talking about me behind my back to one of my friends?" I breathe in through my nose. "I trusted you. I looked up to you. I thought you were my friend. And you had to go and screw it up."

I turn to go, but he grabs my shoulder. "Adam, please. It's just..." He pauses and I stare at him, hoping, praying that maybe this whole thing is just a bad dream. Hoping hoping hoping with everything that I have that maybe this is all just some big mistake and maybe I misheard him or maybe I'm overreacting.

But no one's that lucky.

"What? What is it?" I hiss.

"You drain me," he cries, throwing his hands up in defeat.

There they are: three little words that have the power to crush anyone.

"I try and I try to be there for you, but I don't know how. It's like, you text me that you want to kill yourself and I tell you to get over it and you get all hurt and I just don't understand. I don't understand you. And I'm not perfect. I can't love you the way you want me to. I can't be there for you when you want me to be. I just can't."

I wrench my shoulder away from his grip, nostrils flaring. I lean in and through clenched teeth, I breathe, "All I ever wanted was for you to be there. You didn't have to say or do anything. You just had to be there like you promised."

I start to walk away, but I stop, silent for a moment. Turning around to face him once last time, I try to read the expression on his face, but there's nothing there to read. There's nothing there for me anymore. My mind is going haywire. "You told me I could always come to you and you'd always be there. You told me I would never be a burden. You told me so many things and you made so many promises. I guess that makes you a liar."

He's looking at the tile floor now. "Things change."

I scoff and start to say something else, but I stop myself. He isn't worth it. So I turn away from him. "And I guess that makes me an idiot," I whisper to myself.

And I leave the dorms behind.

And I leave Jeremiah behind.

And everything I was, everything I thought I could be, is scattered all over the floor. And I leave the pieces behind too.

Back at The Canterbury, I realize I'm still looking at Jeremiah and he's still avoiding my gaze. Oliver glances at me and in that split second, I think that maybe I see a sliver of sadness in his gaze. And I almost feel bad, but I remind myself that he made his own choice. No one forced him to walk away. No one forced him to choose one friend over the other.

I'm angry and I try to calm myself, but the pot in my system doesn't help. *At all.* It just makes things worse. My hand is balled up in a fist under the edge of the dining table, fingernails digging into my palm until I feel the familiar warmth of my own blood. My hand is shaking and I'm sweating. And I can't do this anymore.

I can't I can't I can't

I spring from my chair, shove my fist in my pocket and leave the dining hall. I don't care if Garcia doesn't know where I am and I don't wait around for the party to end to get a ride back to the school, so I take a bus.

I can't live like this.

It's like every fiber of my soul is being tugged in different directions, tearing me apart, a tangled thread of sorrow and rage and regret and pain and shame and fear. And *I hope I hope I hope* that love is in there somewhere.

Because without love, what's the point? Without love, every good thing ceases to matter.

I have to get away. Not just away from the Canterbury, but away from everything that reminds me of the person I was once and the person I can never be again.

On the bus now, I feel hopelessly and utterly lost. My heart aches and I feel like I've just been stabbed in the stomach. I stay on the bus for a long time and let it take me wherever it wants. I watch the water droplets cling to the window as they roll to the bottom, where they let go. And I need to let go too, but I know it's not the time.

Where do I go from here?

I think of Liz. I'm lost and I'm in ruins. Everything I thought I was is gone and it hits me now that it's never coming back. And I can't help but think of Liz in the middle of it.

Numb and unable to bring myself to move, I stay on the bus until the driver tells me I have to get out.

I'm standing in the rain now, somewhere in the middle of San Francisco. It takes me a while to figure out where I am and when I do, I button my jacket, pull my collar up around my neck, and walk back to the school. Through the rain. Through the darkness and the flickering streetlights. Invisible and tired and a little bit angry. But there's nothing I can do about it.

I push through.

6

Drenched. Sweat, tears.

Bruised. Sore, bleeding.

I can't breathe. I'm on the floor and my eyes won't open. There's a sharp pain in my side. Mom is screaming and I hear the sound of something heavy hit the floor beside me.

Finally, my eyes open and I see him. Standing over us. Towering. Angry. Holding his beer tightly like he always does.

So much anger. So much rage in his eyes. He's yelling something, but I don't hear it.

Dad, *I try to say, but nothing comes out.*

He wouldn't listen anyway. He never does.

Mom is on the floor, writhing, weeping, afraid. So am I. But I slid to where she is and throw my body over hers, taking the last of Dad's anger on myself.

It burns. Something cracks inside of me, sending a sharp exhale from my lips.

But I'm frozen. I stay here. I can't let him hurt Mom anymore. She needs me.

It will end. Soon. It never lasts long. And tomorrow will be better. He'll wake up in a better mood. He'll be happier. And he'll apologize for losing his temper and Mom and I will smile at him through cracked lips and sore eyes and we'll forgive him.

We always do. Because it's Dad.

It's family.

Family loves. Family forgives. Family sticks together. Right?

I skip classes Thursday and stay in my room all day, not bothering to even shower. And I don't leave my bed except to use the restroom.

Liz texts me, asking why I ditched and I tell her that I wasn't feeling well. Because that's what you do. You give people excuses that keep them from worrying. That keep them comfortable. Because you don't want to make people uncomfortable with the truth. The truth breaks you.

It broke me.

The rest of the day is empty and before I know it, day begins to turn to night. But before the darkness comes, I pull myself from my bed long enough to leave the dorm and climb onto the roof. It's cold and I didn't bring my jacket out with me, but the bite of the evening chill is strangely comforting. I face the sunset, watching the light fade from me. I can feel it, too. I try to hold onto it, the warmth and the brilliance, but it leaves me. Isn't that the way it goes? The light always leaves no matter how much you don't want it to.

I suppose that's all the more reason to enjoy the light while it's here. I do just that and then, I notice that, even though I'm in the center of the city and I'm surrounded by artificial light and the sun is gone, the stars seem especially bright tonight.

It's a funny thing. Even the darkness seems brighter since I met her.

Friday.

I abandon my room in time to make it to my classes, where I see Liz. She walks over and sits beside me this time and my heart beats a little faster. "Feeling better?" she asks.

"Much," I say with a nod.

"Good." She plops her backpack down on the table in front of us and proceeds to pull her laptop out. "How about we walk the track after classes?"

I look up at her. "That sounds perfect." What she doesn't know is that the track, a gravel path that circles the field in the middle of campus, used to be one of my favorite places to go. She smiles just as the professor walks to his podium and begins roll call. This class is particularly boring, but maybe that's because I'm distracted, watching Liz out of the corner of my eye.

After class, we take our things to our rooms and meet outside the dorms. Following the sidewalk, we come to the track and step onto the gravel.

It's overcast, cloudy. "When I was a kid, my dad and I used to lay down in the grass in our backyard and look up at the clouds and find shapes and pictures. It was one of my favorite memories." A blink. "What do you see?" I look up, pointing.

We watch them on the horizon and above us, finding

the pictures and shapes in them and calling them out by name.

"That one looks like a Unigator."

"A *Unigator?*" I chuckle.

"Yeah! It's a cross between a unicorn and an alligator."

"That doesn't count."

"Sure it does," she protests.

I just laugh and we go on like this. After a while, though, she has to leave for an appointment with her academic advisor. I walk her back to the sidewalk and as she walks away, she turns her head and gives me a smile. "Bye. Thanks for the walk."

I smile and give a short wave. "No. Thank *you.*"

With that, she leaves.

I don't think I could ever forget her smile.

Saturday, Sunday, Monday all pass in a blur, fragments in my head until they all jumble together and I can't tell one from the other. I haven't seen Liz since our walk Friday. Finally, I get to see her again in class on Tuesday morning. She's a little late, so we don't get to talk before the professor starts roll call. But when she gets to class, she smiles and waves at me and I smile and wave back. I avoid Jeremiah like the plague and I don't look at him even though, out of the corner of my eye, I can see his head turned toward me. There's no more room inside of me for the weight of his judgment.

When class is over, Liz and I meet just outside the classroom door and I walk with her back to the dorms.

"So what do you do in all your free time? You seem to spend a lot of time in your room," she asks.

"I write," I say. "I keep a journal." And I don't know why, but I add, "I used to write music too. And play."

She widens her eyes. "Really?"

I nod.

"You'll have to play for me some time."

I shrug. "I don't think I could. I haven't played in a long time. I'm probably no good anymore."

She scrunches her face and narrows her eyes at me. "Okay, well, maybe someday."

"Maybe. Someday."

Wednesday.

I get lost in the days, now. The hours and the minutes and the seconds consume me until I can't tell the moments apart. I spend almost all of my free time with her so I haven't written in my journal the last few days.

Today is Wednesday, I remind myself. *Right.*

I can't tell where I am right now. Mentally, that is. My mind constantly wanders to Liz and with each passing second, I feel myself floating higher and higher until everything around me is gone and it doesn't matter. But then I see Jeremiah in passing or I see him from a distance and I come crashing down. I hate that it's that easy.

I look over at the pantry in my room and I see it. My guitar, propped up in its stand. I never got to use it at the Christmas Festival. I couldn't even go after what Jeremiah said. But I still remember where I was when I was supposed to be performing. I was on the floor of the shower, surrounded by my own blood as it was swept down the drain. I remember not being able to breathe as the tears and the blood mingled with the shower water, as I hyperventilated. Thanks to the icy water, I didn't feel the sting of the open wound on my chest over my heart. I was numb.

I haven't touched my guitar since the moment Jeremiah stopped believing in me. Because in that moment, I stopped believing in myself too.

Why? I ask myself with every burning memory of him. *Why do I let myself remember someone who so easily forgot about me?*

I don't want this. I don't want this hurt. I don't want this destruction. I don't want this stinging in my chest every time I think of someone I used to know.

Suddenly, there's a resolve that constructs itself inside my chest and I inhale deeply. I remember that this is *my* life. *I* make the rules. I will live and die on *my* terms. And right now, I want to live because the thought of her doesn't escape me. I'm not happy just existing. I'm not happy just surviving.

I want to *live.*

Alone in my room, I smile to myself at the thought of her.

I turn a few pages back in my journal and find the entry from two weeks ago.

I need to know her.

And those words become real to me again. I feel them

in my bones now.

Before I can stop myself, I'm moving. I grab my backpack and shove some clothes and the other things I can't live without (phone charger, journal, deodorant, and toothbrush) inside without any particular order.

And then I walk over to where my guitar is. A thin layer of dust coats it and I pick it up by the neck. I sit back down on the chair and, with trembling hand, pull the guitar closer, resting it on my knee. I grab a napkin and gently dust it off. When I'm done I open my desk drawer and pull out a pick. I freeze when it gets closer to the string.

I don't know if I can do this. I don't even know if I can play anymore.

What have I got to lose?

So, taking a deep breath, the fingers on my left hand find their place and, gripping the pick, I begin to strum.

And I think I start to cry as the music fills my room. But I stop myself and shove my pick in my pocket. I grab my backpack and, guitar in hand, I leave my room.

I walk across the dorm floor and don't let myself stop when I see Jeremiah's name on his door. I keep going until I pass it and then I'm outside and across the parking lot and shoving my things inside the back of my van.

Breathless, I pull my phone from my pocket and turning it on. I move to my contact list and my thumb hovers over her name until I press it, as if those three letters can keep me grounded, keep me sane.

I type without thinking, my thumbs flying across the on-screen keyboard.

ME
Let's go.

A few minutes later, she texts back.

LIZ
Where?

ME
Nowhere. Everywhere. It doesn't matter. Let's get lost.

LIZ
OK

And that's all I need.

ME
OK

7

In life, there are losers, there are winners, and there are participators. My entire life, I've fallen into the third category. But I will *not* be satisfied with being a participator anymore. *So,* I decide, *I will win. If not tomorrow, then at least for today.*

Naturally, I'm in front of the girls' dorm now, knocking wildly on the glass door until Amy answers, her hair a matted mess.

"Adam?" She blinks, whining, "I was taking a nap."

"Can you get Liz for me?"

"Sure," she mutters, disappearing back into the dorms.

I wait until Liz walks out a minute later, wearing the smile that is forever burned into my mind. I only have a vague idea of what I'm doing, but that's okay. Because I'm here, in this moment, now, with her. And that is the one thing in the world that matters right now.

"Where to?" she asks, anticipation brooding in her eyes.

"The adventure is in the not knowing," I say with a wink.

With a roll of her eyes, Liz crosses her arm and shakes her head, laughing a little. "*Vague* must be your middle name."

"Actually, it's Zachary."

"Adam Zachary West? I like it."

I smile. "I'll wait with Gus while you grab whatever you need."

She furrows her brow, confused. "What do I need?"

I shrug. "Clothes, blanket, pillow, and whatever else you can't live without."

"What about school?"

"What *about* school? I, for one, am not gonna let tomorrow keep me from living today." I throw my hands out to my sides. "Live a little! We've only got so long." I grin.

She hesitates for a moment and I know this is a lot to ask of someone I've known for a few days, but still I wait, *hoping hoping hoping...*

Finally, "Okay. I'll be right back," she says, a spark in her eye, and disappears behind the glass door.

Sighing, I run my fingers through my wild hair, scratching at my scalp as I walk over to where Gus is parked. I climb into the driver's seat and Gus roars to life when I turn the key. "No trouble for me today, eh, buddy?" I pat the dash affectionately.

Liz makes her way toward us, toting a brown pack. I hop out of the van and walk over to the passenger side, sliding the door open so she can toss her pack in next to mine. Glancing down at her, she turns to meet my gaze and smiles up at me.

"We've only known each other a couple of weeks and I'm pretty sure this is a bad idea, but...," she says, folding her arms into her chest.

"All the best adventures start with bad ideas. Besides, when it's all over we won't be strangers anymore. Maybe you'll finally get to know the anomaly that is Adam West."

"You're not an anomaly, Adam."

I smile. "There is much you've yet to learn about me."

"That's the point. I am getting ready to go God-knows-where doing God-knows-what with a veritable stranger."

"What I'm hearing is that the perfect opportunity to get to know each other just fell right into our laps." I wink. "Besides, how many people that you *actually know* even say that you can't go on a joyride with a guy who's clearly into you?"

She blushes, then laughs, tongue-in-cheek. "Alright," she whispers, then again louder and more confident, "Alright. Let's do it. What've we got to lose?"

"Atta-girl!" I shout, holding the passenger door open for her. She steps in and I close it shut.

I walk around the front and jump into the driver's seat.

As I shift Gus into gear, I glance over at Liz and, with a grin, I say, "Let's make some waves." And then we're off.

8

The sun begins to set now. Liz and I have spent the last few hours just driving.

At some point, Liz announced, "We're gonna play 20 Questions." And at some point, I think we exceeded the twenty-question limit.

"What's your favorite color?" she asks.

"Black," I answer. "What's your middle name?" My phone plays *Fall Out Boy* in the background and my fingers tap the steering wheel to the beat of the music.

"I actually don't have a middle name."

"Really? Is there a story behind that?"

"Not really," she shrugs. Out of the corner of my eye, I see her lean into the corner between the seat and the door as she props her feet up on the dash. Inwardly, it makes me happy to know she feels like she can relax around me.

"C'mon. There's gotta be a story behind something as socially anti-norm as not having a middle name."

"Well, my parents used to be hippies and when I was born they didn't want to subject me to the confusion that comes with having multiple identities. Friends and family call you by your first name or a nickname. Most parents say your full name when you're in trouble. Teachers call you by your last name. And so on. But my parents? They just wanted one identity for me. Something like that, anyway."

"See, I told you there was a story." I smile at her.

She laughs. "It's a story that doesn't make sense, but sure. What's your favorite song?"

"See, now that's an impossible question to answer. Music is the lyrical breathing of the wandering soul. But every breath tells a different story. So how can I choose just one? How can I choose one breath over all the thousands of breaths I've ever breathed? How can I choose just one?" I find myself yearning for the days when I wrote music myself. I miss those happier times when it was just me, my guitar, and my music. But those days are gone now.

"I don't think that counts as an answer," she laughs.

"Okay. For now, I'll choose 'Awake My Soul.' *Mumford and Sons.*"

"Good choice," she says.

"Good song," I say.

"Play it."

I hand her my phone and she scrolls through my iTunes library until she finds the right one and it begins to play. We drive into the orange glow of a tunnel, basking in the music as it floods the atmosphere inside the van. In the afterglow, I feel so very deeply what the song is saying. I feel the lyrics inside me, filling me, becoming me. And I wish that I wasn't driving just so I could feel Liz's fingertips against mine again. I begin to question everything I'd ever thought I needed. I begin to question my future and plans. Because with her, now, here beside me, this moment is all I need. This is all I want. I know now that I would spend an eternity bearing this pain if it meant I might sit beside her for just a day.

Just a day is all I need. Just a day to feel alive.

Just a day...

I turn off the road. The world is bathed in night now and we're in the middle of nowhere – the empty space between cities and towns.

I drive onto the beach and park in the middle of the sand.

I slip my shoes and socks off and open the door. I slide out of my seat and let my feet sink into the still-warm sand. Walking to the other side, I slide the back door open, pulling out a blanket. My eyes linger on my guitar a moment before I grab it and swing the strap over my shoulder. Then, I open her door and extend my hand to her. She smiles and folds her hand into mine.

"Let's go," I say, nodding toward the water.

"You brought your guitar," she says, her eyes bright.

Saying nothing, I just smile.

She follows me, her hand in mine, as close to the water as we can get without stepping onto the wet sand. I spread the blanket out and lie down and she lies down next to me.

We lay there, silently, watching the stars spin their dance. I am here. And Liz is here. We exist in the empty spaces. We exist in the blank pages of journals waiting to be filled. We exist in the spaces no one notices. And we notice them. Because we *are* the empty spaces. And we are the blank pages, the stories waiting to be told. And here on the shore, we write our story. Just me and her, empty pages with hearts of ink, writing each other.

"It's my turn," I say. "Who's your favorite poet?"

"*Some people talk and talk and never say a thing*," she recites, "*Some people look at you and birds begin to sing. Some people laugh and laugh and yet you want to cry. Some people touch your hand and music fills the sky.*" She turns her head to me. "Charlotte Zolotow."

We lie here, watching each other, listening to the orchestra of the waves beyond us. My fingers find hers, but I don't grab hold of her hand. Not yet. I just linger there, our fingertips barely touching and I feel the electricity between us. "Do you hear it? The melody of the stars and the night – of the wind and waves? Do you hear them singing for us?" I whisper.

She blinks then nods, slowly. "Adam," she says my name as though it were a thing to be lost. A moment later, "The only song I want to hear right now is yours." Brave are words like those. Brave are hearts that ask, that open themselves up to vulnerability, that make themselves known, truly known.

My heart skips a beat and I smile, sitting up. I reach for my guitar and pull it to my lap. My memory goes to the song I wrote for the Christmas Festival.

Inhaling, I begin to strum, to sing, and it feels like I've come home.

Liz is completely still as she listens to me and I keep singing, my eyes fixed on her moonlit eyes. The music surrounds us and carries us until we're in our own little world with a population of two. Everything, everyone else falls away.

"That was beautiful," she whispers when the music fades. It's only now that I see the mist in her eyes.

I set my guitar on the sand beside me and lay back down. "It's been a long time," I breathe.

"Thank you," she says.

I look over at her. "No. Thank you."

We lie there a moment, staring up at the stars. In my heart, I'm reaching and I think there's a part of her that's reaching too. It's magnetic.

It's gravity.

"What's your favorite poem?" she asks.

"*My soul is full of longing for the secret of the sea, and the heart of the great ocean sends a thrilling pulse through me.* Henry Wadsworth Longfellow."

Silence. Then, "You have a thing for the ocean, don't you?" she breathes.

"Yeah."

"Why?"

"Because it's as wild and endless as I feel."

We linger here in the empty spaces and there is no void between us.

I roll onto my side and rest my hand on her cheek. I trace her cheekbone with my thumb and tuck a loose strand of hair behind her ear. And in that moment my body is no longer my own. I am a passenger of want.

I kiss her.

But then she's pulling away and my heart is frozen. She presses her hand to my chest and gently pushes me from her, our lips breaking contact.

"I can't," she says and I don't know what she means.

"I'm sorry, I-"

"No," she shakes her head wildly. "It's not you." But that's it. She's on her back again, staring up at the brilliant sky.

I roll onto my back too and I think I've lost. But before I can start to spiral out of control, her fingers find mine again. I know there's something there. I know it as deeply as anyone can know anything. And even though we're not quite holding hands, we fill the atmosphere with something strange and electric.

My heart beats loud, burning inside its cage. Blood races through my veins and I can hear it pulsing in my ears. I think, maybe, I hear hers too. Beating, pulsing, humming.

We lie here, our wildly and truly being, one beside the other, filling the empty spaces with the sound of us. Demanding to be heard, shouting into the void, *"We are here. We exist. We matter."*

And under the starlight... here and now... with her, I feel endless.

9

The sound of the waves greets me as I wake.

It takes me awhile to open my eyes and I stretch as they adjust to the brilliant morning sun. At some point last night, we crawled into the back of the van and curled up under a blanket. Together. Liz still sleeps beside me, the back of her head nestled into the crook of my shoulder. Her hair covers the side of her face, so I pull it back behind her ear and just lie here, watching her sleep, her breath slow and rhythmic. It all seems so surreal.

A loud tapping on the door startles me and Liz snaps awake. I open the door to see a police officer standing over us. "Yessir?" I ask, my voice groggy.

"Does this look like a hotel to you?"

"No, sir."

"You kids need to leave. You're trespassing on private property."

"Sorry, Officer. We'll go."

"Good. I don't want to catch you here again. You hear me?"

"Yes, sir."

He narrows his eyes at me. "Alright. Drive careful."

"Thank you, sir."

He walks back to his patrol car and I hop out, moving

around to the driver's side and turn the key until the engine starts. Liz climbs up into the passenger seat and I shift Gus into gear and drive off of the beach and back onto the road.

Liz starts laughing.

"What's so funny?" I ask, eyebrow raised.

She laughs harder and then I start to laugh too. It doesn't make sense, but it feels good.

Finally, after a long time, we catch our breath.

"Where to next?" Liz asks.

"Have you ever been to Point Reyes?"

"No, I haven't. What is it?"

"It's a national park out on the coast and there's this tiny, beat up, old lighthouse that just sits on this cliff. I mean, it's been restored, but you can tell that it's seen a few storms. But the thing is, you have to climb up a hill and then you haven't even reached it yet because it's at the bottom of over 300 stairs. And it's like you climb all the way down just to see this tiny, beat up, old lighthouse and then you have to climb back up those 300 stairs and back down the hill.

"But, see, most people don't appreciate that tiny, beat up, old lighthouse. Most people are disappointed when they get down there to see that it's not spectacular, it's not noteworthy. It just *is*. But what they don't get is that this tiny, beat up, old lighthouse is just as important as any of those spectacular, new ones that are super easy to get to. Because it doesn't matter what year the lighthouse was built, or how big it is, or any of that. All that matters is that this tiny, beat up, old lighthouse brought ship after ship after ship safely to harbor."

I look at Liz, who just grins at me. "I think that this tiny, beat up, old lighthouse should be a national monument, a memorial to every shipwrecked soul whose life was saved by the lighthouse nobody noticed."

"But the people who matter noticed," Liz says. "The people lost at sea, they noticed." She looks at me, a smile dancing on her sky-blue eyes.

"That, they did," I say.

So I drive north until we reach Point Reyes National Seashore. We park in the guest parking and make our way up the hill.

"This isn't so bad," Liz says, controlling her breaths step by step.

"We haven't gotten to the stairs yet." I wink at her.

She sticks her tongue out at me and darts up the hill. "Race you to the top!"

I laugh and watch her go for a minute before starting off after her. Passing an older couple, I nearly bump into the man. "Sorry!" I shout back at them. He just waves me off and I keep racing up the hill, careful not to slip on loose gravel.

Liz reaches the top of the hill first and turns to me. Then she disappears into one of the juniper trees that line the path as it twists behind the face of the cliff. I catch up with her just as she starts to climb the tree and disappear into its branches. So I step onto the lowest branch and climb after her.

"Careful!" she calls down. "The branches are slippery."

Heeding her warning, I climb slowly until we're on the

highest branch. She sits down, straddling it with both her legs and I sit down across from her. Below us, the hillside descends into the obscurity of the morning fog.

Liz watches the world below us, eyes wide with wonder. "It's so beautiful," she says, "so perfect."

"Yeah," I say, but it's not the ocean that has arrested my attention. I sit here, completely and utterly lost for words, captivated by the girl sitting across from me. I study every curve and line of her body. My eyes trace the veins in her hands, pale from the cold of the early morning. Her fingers play with the bark on the branch, tearing a piece off and throwing it to the wind, watching it float gently to the ground.

We sit here, completely silent, and it's enough just to share a branch with her.

I pull my keys out of my pocket and begin to carve my initial into the tree. It's supremely disfigured, but an A begins to form in the meat of the wood. Liz watches me and when I am done she takes my keys from me and carves a + and an L.

And I just watch her as she encircles our initials with half a heart and then she hands my keys back to me and says, "Finish it." And so I do. I complete the heart and shove my keys back into my pocket and we admire our perfectly imperfect work of art together with all its jagged edges and disfigured lines.

"Now we have something no one can ever steal," she says. "We have our own little part of the world, of history, and even though no one else knows it's here, we will. Always."

"Always," I say. And I know what she means. So much has been stolen from me, but now I begin to wonder... what's been stolen from her?

"So," she says, a grin tugging at her lips, "let's go see this tiny, beat up, old lighthouse of yours." She slides down off the branch and onto the one below, winding her way back to the soft grass with surprising ease. Following, I land beside her and nearly fall as my feet sink into the wet ground. She grabs my jacket sleeve and holds me steady.

holds me steady

We make our way around the corner of the mountain, side by side. Her knuckles brush against mine and then retreat. She does this again, walking close enough beside me that our shoulders brush against each other, then far enough apart that we don't even touch at all. And then she takes my hand in hers and we walk together until we reach the top of the stone-carved staircase.

"Wow, you weren't kidding when you said it was a long way down," she says with disbelief, eying each step.

"No, I was not." I start down the stairs and turn around, extending my hand to her. She takes it and we descend together, single-file, into madness spurred by curiosity and a hunger for every wonderful thing.

It takes us awhile to reach the bottom and as we go, Liz counts the steps aloud. We stop every now and then to admire the view from different vantage points. By the time we finally reach the bottom, our legs are sore from the strain. Liz bends over and massages her calves.

"That was more than three hundred," she huffs.

"Eh, it was a rough estimate." I laugh. I take a deep breath, then, pointing at the lighthouse, proclaim, "There she is."

"Wow," she says, straightening.

We approach it, climb onto the upper deck, and walk around to the part that overlooks the ocean. And we just stand there, leaning against the railing, watching the tossing of the waves.

Liz leans her head on my shoulder and whispers, "It's so calm."

"It's endless," I say, breathless to the point where my voice is barely a whisper, "the cosmic dance of the sun and moon. The magic in their pull brings the sea to life and the sea is helpless to resist them."

"You," she says, "are going to be a poet someday. Or a writer. Or both. You're going to change the way people see the world."

I smile and lean my head against hers. "Someday. Maybe."

"Don't you trust me?" she says, her tone coy.

"Liz, strange as it may sound, right now I trust you more than anyone else in the entire world."

She smiles against my shoulder and we stand there for a little while longer, watching the ebb and flow of the distant sea.

When we finally reach the top of the stairs, we collapse onto a bench and I massage my throbbing legs.

"Was it worth it?" I ask, heaving.

She lies down across the bench and lets her head fall on my lap. "Yes!"

"Good." I take a breath. "We have closed," I gasp, "the BRUTAL DISTANCE!"

"What?" she asks with a laugh, her face screwed up in a mixture of amusement and curiosity.

My lungs still burning, I take a second to steady my breathing, then explain, "The poet Edward Louis Anthony said once, 'I have closed the distance and crossed many seas. There's glory in the wandering and beauty in brutality; this wonder spans the deep.' Anthony was saying, I think, that the things worth achieving are the things we must work for. And they are not near to us; they are far, far away. They aren't easy and it takes struggle, but there is beauty there. It is through the mire of brutal existence *only* that we may come to attain the things worth achieving."

She rolls her head toward the stairs. "No kidding."

We sit here for a while, watching people as they go by.

"Let's play a game," I suggest. "For each person that passes us, we have to create a narrative."

"Ok. You go first, Mr. Writer."

A young girl (probably in her early twenties) walks by. Her hair is black with some red mixed in and her fingernails are painted to look like a rainbow. Her arms are crossed over her chest and as she walks by, her head down, she tugs her denim jacket tighter around her shoulders. She's walking away from the lighthouse, but somehow the stairs haven't winded her like they did us.

"That girl – her name is Serena," I say, nodding to the

black-haired girl, "just broke up with her boyfriend – no, girlfriend – down at the lighthouse, but she didn't want to. She had to because her family wouldn't accept that she was in love with a girl and she's too afraid to disappoint them. She's also a singer and performs weekly at a bar in downtown San Francisco where she hopes to one day make it big as a solo artist. And her favorite food is pizza."

"Okay, okay," Liz says. "My turn." She shifts her head in my lap and scrunches her face up, attempting to conjure a story within the confines of her beautiful, *beautiful* mind as an older couple walks past us, toward the stairs, each held on their feet by a pair of canes. The woman leans on the man and they take the steps slowly, together, until they disappear.

"Her name is Phyllis and his name is George and it's their 60th anniversary. They made each other promise decades ago that when they got old they would never stop going on adventures. So they're here, making good on that promise, commemorating decades of dedication and love and adventure. And they have three children together and fourteen grandchildren and seven great-grandchildren. And tomorrow they're going to catch a flight to Miami where they'll move in with their oldest son and his wife until they die, happy, together, loved."

As she says all this, I listen, and I imagine that this is us 60 years from now, together, happy, and forever wild at heart, two souls beating as though they are waves that can never be tamed.

We play this game for a long time until Liz says, "I'm

hungry." So we stroll back to where Gus is parked and drive to the nearest McDonald's.

"We should head back to campus," Liz says, shoving a handful of fries into her mouth and taking a sip of her milkshake.

I look up at her, but don't say anything.

"My phone is almost dead, I need a shower, and we can't miss too many classes. Otherwise people are gonna start asking questions."

"People will ask questions anyway." I shrug. "Humans, they like to make assumptions, regardless of how unfounded they may be. It's in their nature. Besides, you and I both disappearing without a word on the same day? That isn't exactly inconspicuous."

"Which is why we should go back. So we can put to rest any unwelcome rumors."

The truth is, I couldn't care less about what anyone else thought was going on. I stopped caring weeks ago. But I know Liz is right. "Okay, we'll go back soon," I say. "But there's one more place I want to show you."

"Where?"

"How about the Golden Gate Bridge? You've been here two weeks and haven't seen it yet. That's just wrong."

"Sounds like a plan," she says, dipping a fry in her milkshake and popping it into her mouth. "I've always wanted to see the Golden Gate Bridge."

"Great. But first, I need to stop and get some gas. Gus is running on empty."

"Poor Gus," she says.

"Poor Gus," I say.

10

By the time we get to back to San Francisco, the sun is already setting. Light floods the sky in waves of pink and gold, mixing with deep blue. Strolling across the bridge, it takes us thirty minutes just to get halfway across. That's where we stop.

Liz leans on the railing and looks out over the bay. "I love it here," she says, turns to me. "Thanks for showing me this."

Smiling, I lean into the railing beside her, close enough that our shoulders barely touch. "You're welcome." Seeing her so amazed by the bridge when, for me, it's become a part of my everyday life... it renews my own love of this city. Seeing her at all, it renews me.

She turns to look at me, eyes searching. "You know, when I first moved here, I was scared. LA has been home for a long time, but there's a lot I was leaving behind. Not just good things." She swallows. "Letting go of all of that and coming here, it was big. But from the first day I showed up, you were there. You made me feel welcome. Not just that, you've made this city start to feel like it could be home." She looks back out at the bay, out at the sun as it disappears. "Adam, everything I left behind, it all leads to you."

I say nothing. Not because I can't find the words, but

because this isn't my moment. This is hers and I won't take that from her. The need for openness is there, hanging on her lips. But inside, I remember how just two weeks ago I was on the other side of this railing, hanging above the end of my life. And now, here I am, looking down at this girl who could easily be the most important person I've ever met in my life.

But it scares me. Because every time I get close to someone, it ends up broken. This thing with Liz, it's making everything new inside of me, but there are some things that even she can't touch.

"Thank you, Adam. Thank you for all of this." And she hugs me.

My heart stops inside of me and my arms forget how to move as she folds herself into me. When I remember how, I hug her back.

And the sky explodes as the last of the sun vanishes behind us.

By the time we get back to campus, it's well past midnight. Everyone's likely fast asleep in their rooms, which is fortunate because it'll be easier for us to sneak inside.

Parking, I turn Gus off and we sit there for a long time.

"Thank you," Liz says finally.

"You've said that already," I laugh. "A couple of times, actually."

She laughs. "I know, but still... I'd forgotten what it was like to just be free, beyond the walls of a life that have been constructed for me by everyone but myself."

I smile at her. "You're welcome."

She opens the door to get out and just as she's about to close it behind her, she says, "To be continued?"

"Yeah," I nod. "To be continued."

She leaves and disappears inside the girls' dorm, but I stay just a little while longer.

I'm falling. But then, I've always been falling, descending into a cavern deeper than my eyes can see. But I've grabbed hold of something, a ledge that wasn't there before, and I'm holding on. I'm holding onto those three little words. And they're not the ones you might expect. They're simple, completely uncomplicated, but they're a promise.

"To be continued," I whisper to the empty seat beside me.

11

He's angry again.

But it's different. It's not just anger. It's rage. It burns in his eyes as he downs the last of the beer in his bottle. He throws the empty glass at me. I lift my arms just in time to protect my head from the blow. The glass shatters, cutting into my arm, forcing a cry of pain from my lips.

"Dad! Please! Don't do this!"

In a rage, he grabs me by the throat and shoves me against the wall.

I can't breathe.

"I am in charge here. Not you. If you ever disrespect me again, I'll beat you senseless."

The smell of alcohol on his breath turns my stomach.

I can't breathe.

I can't even remember what set him off this time.

Mom stands behind him, weeping, shouting, shaking uncontrollably. And I remember. Dad was yelling at Mom for I-don't-know-what, so I stepped in to stop him. Now I'm his target.

Helpless. I'm helpless, a limp ragdoll in the hands of an angry man. There's nothing I can do.

He punches the side of my face, breaking the skin. Deeply. I know because the blood spills into my eyes, blinding me. And I think I'm crying too. Something breaks inside of me and, with everything I have, I slam my fist into his stomach. He reels backward, stunned. Eyes wide with surprise, but the anger returns quickly. I'm still trying to catch my breath when he lunges for me. I jump to the side just in time for him to slam against the wall and stumble onto the floor, head bleeding.

I'm on him in an instant, chest pulsing. I'm thankful that he's drunk because that's the only advantage I have over his 200 pounds of muscle.

With a shout, my fist slams against his face. His arms claw at me, but can't find a grip. I punch him again. And again. And again.

And again.

Until his eyes are swollen shut.

Until he stops fighting back.

Until I can't hear Mom screaming anymore.

Until I can't breathe.

Mom's hands wrap around my shoulders, trying to pull me away. She pulls and pulls until I lose my balance and fall backward onto the floor. Dad's body lies there, unmoving. I wait for what seems like a million light years, watching him, until finally I see his chest rise a little. He's still alive.

I should be happy about that, but I'm not.

Shaking, I start to hyperventilate. What have I done? My hands tremble in front of me, knuckles cracked open, fists covered in blood. I don't feel the pain. Not yet.

What have I done?

Blood and tears burn in my eyes as I stare down at my

father, Mom clinging to him, trying to coax him awake. Why? Why does she care?

Something inside of me breaks as I look at what I've done, who I've become. It was never supposed to be like this. A kid shouldn't have to protect his mother from his own father.

Scrambling to my feet, I look down at Dad one last time just as he tries to scoot himself to a sitting position.

And I run.

12

The weekend goes by in a blur and I make it back to campus just in time for my counseling session with Dr. Keller, which I skip anyway so I guess it doesn't really matter. Dr. Keller isn't real. My relationship with him isn't real. But Liz? Liz is real.

I shoot Liz a quick text.

ME
I'm back.

LIZ
"Out beyond ideas of wrongdoing and rightdoing there is a field. I'll meet you there."

ME
Rumi. Be right out.

I travel the sidewalk until I come to the field. Liz is already out there, lying on her stomach on top of a blanket and as I draw closer I see the book in her hands is a collection of Edgar Allen Poe's complete works. She chews on her thumbnail, staring down at the pages through a pair of glasses.

"Hey, stranger," she says as I lie down on my back next to her.

"Edgar Allen Poe, huh? Favorite work?"

She flips forward a few pages and gives me a sideways glance. "I've read and re-read his works a little more than a few times," she says with a giggle. When she finds the right page, she recites, "*It was many and many a year ago, in a kingdom by the sea, that a maiden there lived whom you may know by the name of Annabel Lee; and this maiden she lived with no other thought than to love and be loved by me. I was a child and she was a child, in this kingdom by the sea; but we loved with a love that was more than love – I and my Annabel Lee; with a love that the winged seraphs of heaven coveted her and me.*"

I smile up at the sky, arms crossed under my head.

"There's more to the poem, of course, but that's the best part, in my humble opinion." She closes the book and rolls onto her side, propping her head in the palm of her hand.

I yank her glasses from her face and set them on my nose, squinting up at the sky.

"Hey!" she squeals and jabs at my stomach with her fingers, I roll away and grab her wrists, wrestling her to the ground. I am on top of her now and we're staring at each other. She smiles up at me, her eyes reaching, daring me. *I want to kiss her.*

I see movement out of the corner of my eye and look up to see Jeremiah walking the trail that circles that field. Our eyes meet, but I quickly look away. Moving off of Liz, I sit back down next to her.

Confused, she turns around. She raises an eyebrow when she sees Jeremiah disappearing down the trail. She looks at me. "What's up with that?"

"It doesn't matter anymore," I say, staring intently at the ground. And it's true, what happened between Jeremiah and me *is* in the past. "He's just someone I used to know." But I can't deny that the hurt remains, a festering wound that even time has proven unable to fully heal.

She puts her hand on mine and leans forward until her head is nearly touching the ground as she tries to look up at me. "Whatever it was, it's over," she whispers. "You're here, now. With me."

"You are absolutely right." I pick her glasses up from the grass and hand them back to her. "You got any more good poems in there?" I point at the Edgar Allen Poe book.

She laughs. "More than enough to last a lifetime."

"Better get started, then." I laugh and roll onto my stomach as she opens the book to where she'd left off and begins to read aloud.

And I just listen.

My *Intro to Philosophy* class Tuesday morning is not nearly as interesting as it usually is, except that the seat next to me is taken.

Liz scribbles furiously in her notebook while Professor Garcia lectures on Gottfried Wilhelm Leibniz and the "Problem of Evil."

As class ends, Garcia says, "Mr. West, if you would please stay behind after class, I have something I wish to discuss with you. Everyone else, you may go. Don't forget that your first essay on the differing views of life after death is due next Tuesday at the beginning of our class. Enjoy the rest of your day."

As everyone starts to leave, Liz shoves her notebook into her pack and says, "Catch you later?"

I nod.

Once it's just Garcia and me, he walks over to me. His short, stocky frame does little to overshadow me, but his expression more than makes up for his body's inability to intimidate.

"Why did you leave the prospective student luncheon? And why didn't you tell anyone where you were going?" he asks.

"I wasn't feeling well."

"Adam, I need you to tell me the truth. Otherwise, I'll have to go to the Dean with this. And God only knows what his reaction will be. But if you tell me why, then *maybe* we can keep this between us." His face softens. Garcia is probably the only professor at this school that I actually like. His classes are always the most engaging and he isn't afraid to talk about every philosophical point-of-view. He challenges me to think, even when not thinking would be easier. And now he's giving me the opportunity to share a burden I've been carrying for a long time and I'm tempted to take him up on the offer, but I keep these secrets for a reason; only I can bear them.

"I can't answer that," I mutter, looking down, arms folded across my chest, my jaw tense.

Garcia sighs. "Have you ever heard the story of the straw that broke the camel's back?

"No."

"It alludes to a proverb that says 'it is the last straw that breaks the camel's back' and means a seemingly minor or routine action can cause an unpredictably large and sudden reaction, because of the cumulative effect of small actions. *But* if you let someone else carry a straw – just one straw – maybe, just maybe, we can work together to make sure this burden doesn't become more than you can bear. But if you don't let me help you, I can't promise that the next straw won't be the last straw."

I say nothing.

"I'm going to give you one more chance, Mr. West. Come by my office Thursday after class if you change your mind." A pause. "You're free to go."

I shove my laptop into my pack and stand to leave, but Garcia grabs my arm.

"Don't be afraid to open yourself up to all the love others may have to offer. Don't be so closed off from everything and everyone else that the light can't get in," he says, his brow furrowed and I think I see genuine concern in his eyes.

"I'm not afraid," I mutter. "I just don't know how. Not anymore."

But the truth is, maybe I *am* afraid.

13

It's happening again. I'm slipping. I can feel myself growing weaker and weaker as each day passes and I can't seem to pull myself from the brink of my own destruction. Oblivion feels inevitable.

I skip Wednesday announcements in the Auditorium and am on the roof of the dorms again, cigarette grasped firm between my fingers as though it were a part of me. And I suppose it may as well be. Though, as I inhale my first drag of the morning, I realize I've gone almost an entire week without a cigarette. The smoke fills my lungs, numbing myself to the chill winds of the world.

Liz texts me: *Where are you?*

I shove my phone back into my pocket and take another drag of the death between my fingers, hoping she'll forgive me later.

At least I know that the one thing I'm good at is destroying myself. I distance myself from everything and everyone I care about, though there is little in this world that fills those spaces in my heart. My soul yearns for the very things that destroy me and I sit back and let the hunger ravish my mind.

The image of Liz smiling, sitting on the juniper tree at

Point Reyes flashes across my mind. I picture our initials carved into the branch and my heart levitates. Then I remember that there's one more thing I'm good at.

I'm good at loving you.

I toss my cigarette to the concrete, crush it, and scurry down the ladder. I climb inside Gus and peel out of the school parking lot.

Our adventure isn't over yet.

Classes are long over so I know that everyone's inside either a) taking a nap, or b) studying. I pace the sidewalk in front of the dorms and send Liz a text.

ME
I'm out front.

LIZ
Be right out.

A few minutes later, she walks out, wide-eyed when she sees me.

Arms out, grin on my face, I present myself to her, dressed in jeans, a white button-down shirt, a thin black tie, and a black blazer. Pressed between my thumb and my index finger is the stem of a long, crimson rose.

She brings a hand to her mouth and I wish she wouldn't do that because all I want right now is to see her smile. But the smile manages to reach her eyes and every other part of her and I can't stop staring. Moving closer until we're only inches away, I lift the rose so that the sweet, flowery scent fills the atmosphere between us. My body grows warm and I say, "Do you, Elizabeth Richards, want to go on another adventure with me?"

"More than anything," she whispers, her eyes drawing me in and I want to kiss her. But I'm afraid and I can't help but think about what Professor Garcia said.

"Good. Do you have a dress?"

"Yeah, of course," she says, her brow furrowed in an adorably thin, tight line.

"Perfect. While you go change, I'll try to get Gus to start."

She leaves and I make my way to the old VW van. Gus roars to life on the first try and I thank him out loud.

Liz walks out and I freeze when I see her. She wears a blue dress that frills out around her knees, the color of the twilight sky. When she gets to the van, she stands in front of me and asks, "What do you think?"

"Stunning," I manage to say. "Absolutely stunning."

Grinning, she twirls. I open the passenger door for her and she steps inside. I give her the rose before slamming the door shut behind her. Hopping into the driver's side, I shift Gus into reverse.

"So where are we going?" she asks, twirling the rose between her fingers, inhaling its fragrance.

"It's a surprise."

"Stop being so vague," she laughs, slapping my arm playfully.

I smile. "Never."

Liz's elbow linked through mine, I guide her into the ballroom of *The Cecil*. Immediately, the dazzling sound of a full orchestra invades our senses and sweeps me away, into another world entirely. A brilliant, high ceiling wraps us in the golden glow of light as it bounces off the bronze finishing. One enormous crystal chandelier dangles from the center of the massive dome, glittering above the array of dancers and musicians.

All across the ballroom, men in tuxedos and woman in extravagant gowns flourish and sway. Turning to Liz, I extend my hand and ask, "May I have this dance?"

Lips pursed in a smile, she says, "I thought you'd never ask."

We glide into the midst of them, she and I.

"One problem," I say, "I don't really know how to dance.

She laughs a little too loud, drawing the stares of a few of the dancers around us. Her eyes widen. "It's okay," she giggles under her breath. "Neither do I."

So we stumble across the granite floor of the ballroom together until, finally, I put an end to this madness. I pull her in close to me, my hand moving to the small of her back, her hand sliding up to my shoulder. And we sway. Slowly, silently, we drift wherever the music takes us. The sound of the stringed instruments pulses through our veins. Our hearts beat with the rhythm of the wind instruments and the percussion.

Liz rests her head on my shoulder as we move gently, drifting further and further from the earth until everything else fades away. We're among the stars, now, and it's just us, adrift among the cosmos. She's the sun and I'm the moon.

And we sway, our hearts grasping at each other with an unequivocal passion. They beat out of the cages within us and I feel the gravity they create, drawing me in and out like a breath, like the tide. And I am helpless to resist the gravity of us.

I can feel the waves around us, *building building building* with the crescendo of the cello. The sea crashes and erupts, wild and free, subject only to us.

And I know with all my heart that I love this girl who is here, leaning against my shoulder. I don't need time to tell me how I feel about her. All I need is the way my heart skips a beat when I see the smile on her lips and in her eyes, or the way I can't stop thinking about her and every moment is consumed by the thought of her, or the way time stands still when I'm beside her. That's all that I need to know that I love her. I breathe her in and I am whisked away, beyond the boundaries of time and space.

And now, we are above it all, just me and her and the stars. The world is at our feet.

The hours glide by and Liz and I sit on the floor against the wall of the ballroom, watching the dancers dance and the singers sing and the musicians weave their melodies into the atmosphere.

I retrieve two glasses of champagne and return to her, offering one of them.

"No, thanks. I don't drink. How'd you get the bartender to give you those, anyway?" she puzzles.

"Twenty dollars can go a long way," I say, taking a sip from one of the glasses. I offer one to her again. "Come on. At least give it a try," I say, offering my most charming smile.

She hesitates, but takes the glass from me. Lifting it to her nose, she makes a weird face. "Here goes," she says, tipping the glass. I watch the shimmering, gold liquid slip through her lips.

Swallowing, she says, "That is... interesting."

I laugh.

Liz leans over and rests her head on my shoulders as I take another drink of my own champagne. We watch the dozens of nameless couples as they move and sway to the music.

Liz slips her hand into mine. "You know, when I'm with you it's like nothing else matters."

I rest my head on hers. "I know what you mean." I kiss the crown of her head. Her fingernails trace the veins on the back of my hand, sending a shockwave through my body.

After a while, we drift from the ballroom and stroll the street outside, surrounded by the solitude of nightfall. Streetlights illuminate the sidewalk.

We walk until we find a bench that stares out across the San Francisco Bay. The moon glistens across the surface of the water, stirring only to the whisper of the wind. The Golden Gate Bridge is a titan in the distance, dark and bleak against the night sky, a withstanding testament to the handiwork of mankind.

"Tell me a story," Liz whispers, leaning on me. She shivers against the January cold so I remove my blazer and drape it around her shoulders.

"*Once upon a midnight dreary,*" I begin, reciting Edgar Allen Poe's infamous work, "*while I pondered, weak and weary...*" The story scatters into the night with the fog, carried by the currents of a gentle wind.

When I'm finished, Liz says, "Let's go to the Grand Canyon."

"Now you're getting it," I say, a smile tugging at my lips. I pull her closer, my arm around her shoulders and we sit for a while before making our way back to Gus.

Later that night, I sit alone in my dorm room, just me and the darkness, pondering Garcia's ultimatum. I can either tell him why I ditched the luncheon or suffer the consequences of going AWOL. And I honestly don't know which is worse. Still, I think that maybe telling someone isn't such a bad idea. And if I don't, I might get suspended and I'm not ready for that to happen yet. Not now. Not when things are finally starting to get a little better.

I text Liz, who probably isn't asleep yet.

ME
We'll leave after classes tomorrow. Need to talk to Garcia.

A few minutes later: *OK.*
With that, I drift to sleep.

14

I wait until after *Intro to Philosophy* when everyone is gone to talk to Garcia.

"Mr. West," he says as I walk up to the podium, gripping the strap of my backpack as if it was a lifeline. "Have you considered my offer?"

I decide to skip the pleasantries and get straight to the point. "I left because I can't stand to be around Jeremiah."

As if expecting more, he raises an eyebrow. So I explain, "I mean, I literally can't stand to be around him. Stuff happened between us and whenever I see him, my chest aches and my heart starts beating really fast and I get sick to my stomach and really anxious and a bunch of other stuff."

He takes a seat. "You're seeing the school counselor, correct?"

I nod.

"What for?"

"Bipolar Disorder, Borderline Personality Disorder, and... PTSD," I mutter, leaving out the part about self-harm and suicidal tendencies.

"And is Jeremiah Jackson responsible for any of this?"

"Dr. Keller says what happened between us indirectly contributed to a break in my mental and emotional state."

"And what was your mental state like before all this happened?"

"Not good." To say the least.

He furrows his brow and gestures for me to sit down. I obey. "I understand that Jeremiah was the upperclassman mentor you were assigned. What happened between you two?"

I can feel my stomach doing somersaults inside me as I try to recall everything that happened between us over my first semester. My mind drifts to the first time I opened up to him.

I hide myself in the shadows of the Admin Building, staring out at the path around the field. I can feel the familiar heat of the tears against my cheeks. I'm shivering, but not against the cold of night. It's something else, something more, something deeper. I can't control it. It's like a knife in my gut, twisting and turning, shredding my insides to pieces. I tuck my knees to my chest, as if somehow they might protect me from the outside.

I can't remember what broke me this time. All I remember is feeling a mix of rejection and loneliness and hurt and worthlessness. A vague, foggy memory comes to mind of me introducing myself to one of my classmates today, which was only the second week of my first semester, and I remember feeling so so so awkward. And the look on their face when I stumbled across my words in a pathetic attempt at social interaction. My face turned red and I didn't know what to do so I just froze and they laughed. They laughed.

And I remember sitting alone through every class of my first two weeks so far, the only one with two empty seats beside him. I tried to introduce myself to people. I tried to be nice. But every time I walked up to someone, something inside of me would freeze and my whole body would shut down until all I could do was walk away. I tried.

I remember it all and it consumes me. But I can't remember if it's real or if it's all in my head. I try to make excuse for them, rationalize it all, thinking that maybe I just misunderstood, but I know the truth. This is who I am. I'm the guy who stays in the back of the classroom that nobody talks to or sits beside. I'm the guy that gets lost in the crowd. I'm the guy that gets picked last for everything.

It's who I am.

And I don't even know why I'm here anymore.

With no roommate to share my dorm with, I can't stand to be in that room alone, so I'm out in the cold night, hidden only by the shadows and the hedge on the backside of the building.

With a trembling hand, I pull the blade from my wallet and watch it glimmer under the glare of the light that illuminates everything beyond me. I don't even think about it; it's become so natural to me. I set the blade to my wrist and let the steel bite into my flesh.

"What are you doing?" someone shout somewhere in front of me.

I startle to my feet and rush to shove the blade into my jacket pocket. Sliding my sleeve back down over my wrist, I stare at the intruder in front of me, a dark silhouette against the orange light.

My eyes adjust and I make out a face in the darkness. It's Jeremiah Jackson, a Junior. I remember him from the mentorship list. He was the mentor they assigned me. But I've never talked to him. I've only seen him around campus and in classes.

"Wha- Nothing," I stammer.

He walks closer, pointing a finger at my wrist. "That was not nothing." I see the concern on his face. "Were you cutting?"

My lips part as if to answer, but no sound comes out. I don't know what to say. Truth be told, I've never been caught in the act. I've always been able to keep it hidden.

After the shock fades, I manage to compose myself. I cross my arms across my chest and say, "Look, it was nothing, okay?"

"What's your name?" he asks, unmoving.

"Adam West."

"You're the kid they assigned me, aren't you?"

I nod.

"Where've you been? Why haven't you introduced yourself?"

"It's not that simple," I say. And maybe it is, maybe it isn't. But it doesn't matter because I don't need a mentor. What would I even do with one? I get by just fine on my own.

"Sure it is. You just walk up to someone and say 'Hi'," he says with a smile.

"Umm..." I'm trapped. Between the wall and Jeremiah, there's nowhere for me to go.

He squints at me, sizing me up. "Oh, you're an introvert, aren't you?"

"I... guess. Yeah." The forwardness of this guy takes me by surprise.

"Well, hey. I get that introverts have a difficult time with social interactions. But I'm your mentor. I mean, that's what they tell me, anyway. So you can come to me with anything. I know my way around campus pretty well – I'm a Junior – and I know just about everyone so just let me know if you need anything. I'm here for you, dude."

"Thanks," I mutter.

He starts to leave, but turns back to say, "One more thing: give me the knife." His face is serious now.

I don't know why, but I listen. I dig it out of my pocket and hand it to him.

He holds it pressed between the tips of his thumb and index finger, as though it were a dangerous creature that might bite back. My blood stains the point and I swallow. All my secrets have been laid out before this stranger, I find myself feeling exposed. Out in the open. Vulnerable.

And I hate that.

"Why do you cut?" he whispers.

I'm silent for a second, remembering my father's body under me, broken and bleeding at my own hands. Remembering the look in Mom's eyes when she pulled me off of him. Remembering the feeling in my chest when I ran away from it all. And remembering everything that happened after that. "It's the only thing I feel anymore." I look at the ground as I say this, my hands balled into fists in my jacket pockets.

He grabs me suddenly and wraps me in a big hug and I stand there, frozen, a deer in the headlights. "Can you feel this?" he whispers into my ear.

"Yeah," I choke.

"You matter, Adam. If whatever's going on in your life causes you to forget everything else, remember this: you matter. To someone, somewhere, you matter."

I'm silent.

He releases me and says, "I'm here for you. Don't be afraid to come to me with anything."

"Okay."

"Okay." He smiles. "Good. I'll see you around." Then he leaves.

"Adam?" Professor Garcia's voice shakes me from my thoughts. "Do you want to tell me what happened between you two?"

I blink. "He lied," I whisper. "He told me he'd be there and he wasn't. He talked about me behind my back. He told me that I *drained* him."

"I'm sorry to hear that." He pauses. "But you can't let one bad experience keep you from living *your* life. You can't punish yourself for Jeremiah's actions. It's not fair to yourself and it isn't fair to those in your life who love you."

I look up at him and I can feel the heat in my eyes as my vision blurs. "I guess that's the problem, then," I say. "I don't think I'm worth being loved."

"Why is that?"

"Look at me!" I say a little too loudly. "I'm a mess! I'm like a tsunami. Wherever I go, people are going to get hurt because I'm unpredictable. One minute I'm happy, the next I can't find the strength to go on and I don't even know why I'm like this. It's like a switch just flips in my head and I start to see everything and everyone around me through this lens of depression and I can't stop it. I want to - *God*, I want to - but I *can't*. And the one person who tried to be there for me couldn't handle it - he told me I wasn't a burden and he lied. He told me he wasn't sick of me yet and he lied. *He lied.*" There's anger and hurt and pain and so many other things in my words now and I feel like screaming. I try to calm myself and look at Garcia, who just listens intently, his brow furrowed.

"I'm so sorry, Adam. You don't deserve that. No one does," he says when I don't say anything else.

I scoff. Maybe it's because I think I do deserve this. I suppose that maybe life has it out for people like me. Maybe we're anomalies the universe never planned for. Maybe people's minds aren't wired to love people like us.

Maybe existence is all I can hope for. Maybe living is too much to ask for.

"Has your counselor talked to you about potentially taking any medication for these things?"

"Yes."

"And are you currently taking any medications?"

"No."

"Why not?"

"I don't have health insurance and I can't afford it."

"I see."

"Look, Professor, I should go. I have a lot of studying I need to catch up on," I lie. I can't remember the last time I studied for any of my classes.

"Alright. We'll talk later, okay?" He stands and offers his hand to me.

"Yeah," I say, shaking his hand.

Just as I turn to leave he says, "Wait."

I turn on my heel. "What?"

"I don't want you to feel like you have to keep things from me. I'm your teacher and I want you to succeed in life. Not just academically, but mentally and emotionally as well. So, please... feel free to come to me for anything. Even if you just need to talk. My door is always open."

I'm so tired of talking about things all the time and never actually taking any real action, but I offer a half smile anyway because I know that's the right thing to do. And because I know Garcia's doing his best. So I say, "Thanks." Then I leave.

ME
You ready to go?

LIZ
I've never been more ready.

15

On the road now, we travel I-80 East after deciding to take the long way through Nevada. *OneRepublic* plays in the background and Liz sits next to me, *rocking out*. I'm laughing so hard because she looks like a drunk monkey and it's the most carefree I've ever seen her.

Here we are, two people who've known each other for four weeks, ditching class again, and traveling the West Coast together, not a single care in the world. We exist outside the walls.

We are wild things.

I make a mental note of how poetic that sounds, promising myself that I'll add it to my journal later.

Swinging her head back and forth, Liz's hair flies in all directions, flicking my arm. I glance at her, the sound of her laughter seeping deep beneath my skin.

We drive for hours, studying the changing scenery and continuing our never-ending round of 20 Questions.

"What do you want to be when you grow up?" she asks.

"This," I say. And it's true. I want to be the carefree, adventurous, bold, wild person that I am when I'm with her. Forever. Always. I want to be like that elderly couple at the tiny, beat up, old lighthouse who never stopped going on adventures, even as their bodies faded.

They never stopped wandering.

They never stopped wondering.

That's who I want to be. I never want this moment to leave me, but I know it will. All good things come to an end. But for now, this is enough.

Night turns to day, giving way to the stars and they are brilliant. There are no cities with their pseudo-light and their pollution to block out the stars tonight. It's just Liz and I and the endless desert.

As we get closer to midnight, I can feel myself growing tired and driving becomes challenging. So I pull off the road and onto the desert terrain (I think we entered Nevada awhile back) and shift Gus into park. Hopping out, I come around to the passenger side and grab a couple of blankets. I sprawl them out on the dry ground and Liz and I lay down together to watch the stars.

The stars are so extraordinarily bright that, without their brilliance, I imagine that the darkness would come crashing down like a tidal wave. I don't think I've ever seen such a brilliant skyscape, such infinite, boundless luminance.

"*A certain darkness is needed to see the stars,*" she whispers beside me.

"Osho."

She nods beside me. In our silence, I wonder why she pulled away when I kissed her all those days ago and I almost ask, but then she's asleep and it's just the stars and I.

Friday morning, we wake to realize we slept outside all night despite the cold. I toss the blankets in the back as Liz climbs into the passenger seat.

"8:43," she says, glancing at the clock on her phone. "My phone's almost dead."

"We'll find a hotel on our way back from the Grand Canyon." Inside, I turn the ignition.

"Good. I'll need a shower too."

I laugh. "Me too."

Gus leaves a trail of dust in his wake as he roars down US-95 South.

Hours later, we pull into the parking lot of the Grand Canyon National Park Visitor's Center and make our way to Mather Point. Aside from Liz and me, there are only a few dozen people here, it still being January and all. I'm thankful that it's not crowded because, frankly, over-crowded parks are the worst.

When we get to the part of the overlook that sticks farthest out into the canyon I am awestruck. Above the canyon, the light of midday fights through the clouds, its rays reaching the earth in lonely beams.

"Wow," I breathe.

"I've always wanted to see the Grand Canyon," Liz whispers, keeping her eyes steady on the view in front of us. "Ever since I was a little girl, it was a dream of mine to see the world." She turns to me, her eyes welling with tears. "Thank you," she says. "Thank you for bringing me here."

She's crying now so I reach out and pull her into my arms because I don't know what else to do. This whole time,

I thought she was mending me. I thought she was helping me find my wonder again. I thought she was reminding me of who I am and who I could still be.

But maybe there are things that have been broken inside of her that I don't know about. Maybe I'm mending her too. Maybe the truth is that we mend each other. And maybe that's how it ought to be.

We spend hours wandering the trails that wind throughout the canyon, admiring every corner of beauty we manage to find. Camera in tow, I'm taking pictures non-stop, but not of the canyon. Of all the wonders in the world, there's only one that makes my heart beat the way it does.

Liz stands on top of a rock overlooking the canyon and poses for me, her hands on her hips and a look of achievement on her face. She tosses me a smile and says, "I have closed," she throws her arms out to the wind, inhales deeply, and shouts as loud as she can, "the BRUTAL DISTANCE!"

Grinning wildly, I lift my camera to my eye and take a picture of her there, arms abandoned, face to the sky.

Grabbing a bystander by the arm, I point to Liz. "That's my girlfriend," I say, mind lost in the complete wildness of this moment.

Puzzled, the stranger just says, "Good for you," breaks free of my arm, and walks away, looking back just long enough to cast me a vaguely annoyed, slightly amused glance.

When I turn back to Liz she looks at me with eyes wide

open, lips parted, but silent. "*Girlfriend?*" she asks, walking over to me.

I take her hands in mine and say, "Liz, you're the *cuttle* to my *fish.*"

"Did you just compare our relationship to a squid?" She gives me a look of disgust.

"I did. *But* you just confirmed that what we have is some kind of a relationship."

"Well, then," she says, squinting at me. Then, "I guess I am okay with that." She shrugs, then tosses me a coy smile.

I wink at her.

Later that evening, we find a cheap motel that should probably be condemned. But cheap is cheap and we're both just broke college students.

I stand on the balcony, leaning against the antique iron railing, looking out across the main street of the smallest, middle-of-nowhere town. The only buildings in the area are a gas station/mini mart, this motel, and a bus station. The street light blinks off and on, over and over, but there are no cars.

Digging into my pocket, I retrieve a half-empty pack of cigarettes. I put one to my lips and light it up. I don't know why I'm smoking right now when Liz is in the room behind me. Maybe it's habit. Maybe it's something else.

As the smoke consumes me, though, I think about what Jeremiah said the first time we talked. "*To someone, somewhere you matter.*"

I've found my someone. I've found my somewhere.

And to her, I matter.

"Can I ask you a question?" I ask. The hotel bed is uncomfortable and I can feel the springs digging into my flesh, but I don't care because Liz is right here in front of me. We sit cross-legged, facing each other, our knees just barely touching.

"Of course," she says.

My cigarette floats between my fingers and I take a drag before saying, "Back at the beach, when I tried to kiss you..." A pause. "Why did you pull away? Did I do something wrong?"

"No, of course not." she says, placing her hand on my free one. Her fingers are light on my skin as she strokes it. She doesn't look me in the eye. She just stares at my hand, studying the veins beneath my skin. It takes her awhile, but finally she says, her voice barely above a whisper, "When I was a kid, my uncle..." she pauses to take a deep breath, as if the truth might suffocate her. "My uncle raped me. Repeatedly."

I don't say anything. I don't do anything. I don't move because I'm afraid that if I do I might scare her off and I want to hear what she has to say. I want to know every raw, ugly, dirty part of her. I want to know.

She scoffs as tears begin to pool in her eyes. "I can't believe I'm even telling you this." She tries to blink the tears away, but they insist on falling. She breathes deeply, over and over again, until she can regain her composure. She looks up at me and stares right into my eyes, right into my soul. "He was the last person who ever... touched me like that. I've never dated, so I've never kissed anyone else." She sighs. "The only memory I ever have of being kissed is because of my uncle and when you kissed me, it just... It brought all those memories back, you know?"

I could never know, but I nod anyway. Because what I do know how it feels to be alone and I don't want her to ever have to feel that way. Never again.

She goes on. "And it scared me because I thought that if you ever found out you wouldn't see me the same way; that you'd see me as used and broken."

"I could never think that." I lift my hand to her cheek and wipe the tears away with my thumb. "I don't want just the beautiful and flawless, perfect and composed parts of you. I don't want just the parts of you that everyone else sees and wants," I whisper. "I want all of you, every part, the ugly and the flawed."

As I hold her face in my hands, she smiles and I feel the weight of her world pressed against my palms. "Maybe, if you'll let me, I can be what you dream about instead."

She gives a slight nod and I lean in. I kiss her forehead and I move my lips down, letting them glide across her face and I kiss just below each of her eyes, where the tears have gathered. I taste the salt of her grief on my tongue.

Then I take her lips in mine and I kiss her. Not deeply, at first. Our lips touch just enough to feel the electricity pass between us. We linger in this moment for what seems like a breathless infinity. Our heads rest against each other and I look into her eyes and she looks into mine.

I see the ocean in her eyes, deep and dark, mysterious and *endless.*

When I pull away, I say, "I'll sleep on the floor."

She nods, lying down on the bed, and I pull the covers over her. I extinguish my cigarette in the ashtray, turn off the lights and lie down on the floor.

I drift to sleep with the taste of her lingering just a little while longer.

16

When I wake, my back is sore thanks to the stiff flooring. Pulling myself up to a sitting position, I stretch, and when I turn my head I see Liz is still asleep. Curled up under the covers, her hair drapes across her face. I sit on the edge of the bed beside her and tuck her hair behind her ear. Everything is quiet and I just watch her. She breathes, softly, shortly – in, out.

Her eyes flutter open and I greet her with a smile. "Good morning," I say, my throat dry, in desperate need of coffee.

She stretches out across the bed. "Good morning."

"Did you sleep well?"

"Nope. You?"

Glancing at the floor, I laugh. "Not at all. I'm going to go take a quick shower and I'll be right back." I stand to go, but she grabs me by the arm.

"No, wait." She looks up at me. "Could you just stay here for a little while?"

I smile. "Of course." Lying down on my side so that I face her she rolls so that she faces away from me and scoots closer until we're wrapped up in each other. I rest my arm around her stomach and feel her breathe against me.

Kissing the crown of her head, inhaling the scent of her hair, we drift off to sleep together.

We're on the road now with about 7 hours left until we get back to San Francisco, but neither of us is ready to go back. We stopped to get gas and food from the mini-mart before we left the tiny pit-stop of a town.

Driving now, I pull a cigarette from my pack and set it between my lips. Lighting it, I take a long drag, welcoming the smoke into my lungs. With a twist of the knob, I roll my window down and exhale the smoke into the wind. In my peripheral I see Liz twirl a cigarette between her fingers, studying it with curiosity and what seems like a vague wariness. "Why do you smoke?" she asks.

I shrug. "I don't know. Because I can? And because everyone tells you 'you shouldn't smoke' and that just makes me want to do it even more." It's only a half-truth, but I stick with the simple explanation. The full truth is much more complicated. It always is. And I have no room for complications in my life. Not now.

"Such a rebel," she says with an amused sigh. Taking the lighter, she gives it a flick with her thumb and presses the flame to the end of the cigarette in her hand. She lets it dangle between her thumb and forefinger a minute longer before setting it to her lips.

She takes a deep breath – too deep for her first try – and sputters, choking on the smoke.

"That's nasty," she wheezes.

Laughing, "It's an acquired taste."

Despite her coughing fit, Liz puts the cigarette back up to her lips and inhales again, this time more gradually. She rolls down her window and blows a cloud of smoke into the desert.

She winks at me and I smile back.

"Where to next?" she asks.

I think for a minute. "*The mountains are calling and I must go.*"

"Who said that?" she puzzles.

"John Muir. He was a Scottish-American naturalist who petitioned the U.S. Congress for the National Park bill that passed in 1890, establishing Yosemite National Park. He's called the 'Father of National Parks.'"

"Yosemite, then?"

I look at her with a grin. "Yep!"

She pulls out her phone and maps our route.

"Geronimo," I say, hunching forward, both hands on the steering wheel as I urge Gus onward. There are no other cars on the road in the middle of the desert, so I push Gus faster and faster until we're going well above the speed limit. The exhilaration floods my bones as Liz's laughter fills the cab of the van.

And at least for this moment – in the middle of the smoke, the music, and the hot desert wind - all of life collides into this great, big sphere of perfect bliss.

We don't get a motel this time. Instead, we just pull off the side of the road and crawl into the back of the van. We huddle under the blankets we brought and I wrap my arms around Liz, pulling her close to me. The January cold bleeds through Gus' walls.

"I believe we were in the middle of a game," Liz says, referring to our never-ending round of 20 Questions.

"Whose turn is it?"

"I have no idea." She rests her hand on my knee, moving her thumb in a slow, rhythmic, circular motion.

"I'll go, then." I take a second to think of a question. "What's your favorite color?"

"That's the best question you could come up with?" she laughs.

"Hey, I'm tired and it's cold so just answer the question!"

"Fine, fine. Umm... Black. But not solid black. More like the color of the sky after the sun has completely disappeared and when the stars are at their brightest. Like tonight."

I glance out the window and into the Nevada desert, enveloped by the deep blue sky and the brilliant glimmer of scattered stars. "Your turn," I say.

"What's your favorite food?"

"There's this pizza place – *Fultano's* – in my hometown in Oregon that's only local to the Pacific Northwest and it's literally the best pizza you'll ever have."

"Mmm.... That sounds good right now."

I nod. "What's your blood type?"

"What on earth?" She raises her eyebrows at me like I'm the craziest person she's ever met. And I probably am.

"Hey, if you ever need, like, a transfusion or something

then at least I'll know your blood type," I insist.

She rolls her eyes. "Fine. O-Negative."

We continue the game until we can't think of any more questions and then we fall asleep beside each other.

After stopping for lunch at a hole-in-the-wall Chinese restaurant, we finally arrive at Yosemite National Park and as soon as I step out, I am blown away by the stunning array of mountain and forest and overcast skies.

We grab our packs, stocked with water bottles and sandwiches from the mini-mart in Nevada, and start hiking.

We follow the winding trails for hours until we feel we've climbed high enough. We stop at a rocky cliff that sticks out over the valley. It's stones on top of stones and there's no railing, but I don't care. I walk right up to the edge and look down at the earth below, where forest and mountain mingle. (Mom would kill me if she saw me right now.)

I stand on the edge of the earth, where everything ends. Where the world has been cut away and the sky swoops down to fill the void. I think that everything could end here, that I could cease to be the Adam I've known. Could I become something else? Do people like me really get moments like this where we stare into the heart of the void, where everything that was and is meets its end, and get the chance to choose between yesterday and tomorrow.

Looking down at the world now, *someday* begins to stir inside of me.

Liz walks up and stands beside me. She takes my hand

in hers and stares into the void with me. There's a distant look in her eyes and I can't tell if it's calm or troubled.

We're all troubled, I think. *What does it matter?*

"I used to think that it wasn't up to us," I say, my eyes fixed on the clouds. "Life, that is." She squeezes my hand gently. "I used to think that people like me – people who've seen the things I've seen, done the things I've done – we only get to exist, subject to the laws of nature. *Only the strong survive,* and *kill, or be killed* and all that. I used to think that I was destined to spend my entire life waiting for a *someday* that would never come. But now," I look over at her, "with you, I think I've found my someday."

She smiles at me. My eyes burn.

I stare out at the clouds again. "I want to shout into the void that I'm here. I want to make sure that the universe knows that I refuse to be satisfied with just existing. I'm going to *live.*" I turn to her and hold her face in the palms of my hand, staring down at her, meeting with the ocean in her eyes. "I've found my *someday*, Liz. And that *someday* is you."

And as we stand on top of the world, I dare to kiss her.

17

The road between here and there is a long one and Liz eventually drifts off to sleep. So, for now, Gus is my sole companion.

On my phone, I open Pandora and select my *Mumford & Sons* station, imagining this is what it feels like to live. It's nothing extraordinary; just me and Liz on our own adventure, savoring the little moments. But these moments are ours and a rare few people can say that about their lives.

These are the moments that make life worth living.

And I smile to myself.

A few hours later, I pull into the parking lot of the school, just as the sun begins to set. It's the last place I want to be, but knowing that Liz is here with me is enough to keep me sane.

"That was fun," Liz says with a yawn, shrugging off the drowsiness.

"I don't want it to end."

She smiles. "Me neither." A pause. "But we should probably do at least *some* studying." She winks.

Sighing, I say, "Yeah, probably. But I'm taking you out to lunch tomorrow."

"Good. I could do lunch."

I laugh just as a heavy rain begins to pour outside. We sit in the van and listen to the sound of the rain as it pellets Gus' exterior, watching the tiny rivers wind their way down the windshield. I button my jacket up and grab my beanie out of my back pocket. I put it on, pulling it over my ears and I open the door, stepping out into the rain.

"What are you doing?" Liz shouts above the storm. "You're gonna catch a cold!"

Not stopping to answer her, I close the door behind me and follow the sidewalk until I come to the field, where large mud puddles have formed, making it nearly impossible to cross without being soaked. But I don't care. The moment I step into the grass, my shoes are soaked as they sink into the earth. I wade through the mud until I come to the platform the school uses for outdoor events. I climb on top of it and lift my head to face the rain.

I observe it, falling down on me, a never-ending torrent sent to quench the dry California earth. I close my eyes and it's like my senses are on fire and I can feel every drop as it falls against my face, rushing across my entire body like a waterfall. I feel the rain and the cold and the bite of wind like ice. I hear the splash of feet as Liz runs across the field and climbs up onto the platform beside me. I see the clouds as they give everything they have to the earth, holding nothing back.

I feel it all.

I feel it all – the thrum of this moment, the vibrancy of life unexpected, and everything in between.

"Do you feel that?" I shout through the downpour.

"Feel what?" she shouts back.

"Everything." I throw my arms out to my side.

"You're so weird!"

I just laugh and smile into the rain. And then Liz takes my face in her hands and kisses me. At first stunned, I quickly melt into it as our hearts move to the beat of the rain.

We run across the field, back to where Gus is parked, and, opening the doors, we dive inside. By now, the parking lot has begun to flood, rainwater rushing toward the drains. I strip free of my soaking-wet jacket and toss it in the back. Liz does the same and we're sitting in our wet t-shirts and jeans as we watch the rain outside.

"Should we try and make a run for the dorms?" Liz asks.

"Probably," I say.

I kiss her quickly across the console and grab the door handle. "Three, two, one, go!" Darting from our seats, we slam the doors behind us and run toward the shelter of the common area in front of the dorms. The rainwater splashes under our feet and I almost slip on the sidewalk, but we manage to make it without injury.

"*I* will see *you* later." I give her another kiss, short and sweet, and dart inside the men's dorms.

Tucked safe inside my room, I strip free of my wet clothes and wrap a towel around my waste, my body aching for a hot shower.

A smile on my face and Liz on my mind, I head to the bathrooms and climb into the shower.

I let the hot water cascade over my bare skin and burn away the cold. Tilting my head back, I massage the water into my face and scalp, feeling the warmth seep deep into my bones. I run my hand over my chest, my fingers noticing the scars that mark me. I trace every fracture, every break of the skin, each a reminder of things I want to forget. My mind travels back to the moment each scar was inflicted. I remember them all too well, the reasons for my pain. I remember the lonely nights spent with only the darkness. I remember the brutal scrutiny forced on me by my own mind. Every flaw, every failure, every imperfection placed under a microscope and thoroughly - ruthlessly - examined.

I remember the rejection by my peers and every morning spent roaming the halls of my school imagining what it would be like to be someone else, to have any life but this one, to be free of the things I can't escape.

Tracing a long scar that cuts right across the left side of my chest, right above the humming of my heart, I remember the moment I pulled the blade from my wallet. My vision had been blurred by tears and I accidentally cut too deep. I had been in the shower and I remember so clearly, so vividly watching what seemed like an impossible amount of blood wash down the drain.

I remember it all. Every moment, every cut of the knife, every betrayal of a friend, every insult of a peer, I remember.

I will never forget the moments and the people that broke me. I will never forget the things that turned me into a shadow of myself. I will never forget because every day I wake I'm reminded of those moments and people as I see the marks they left on my skin. And I see them when I look into my eyes because they are me.

I've always been my own worst enemy, bringing about my own destruction with every lie believed, with every moment of my own vulnerability betrayed by someone trusted, someone loved, with every moment of false hope.

So I can't help but wonder now if I'm only holding onto something that isn't real – if this, too, is temporary. Maybe I'm only standing in the eye of the hurricane. Maybe it's false hope that tells me I've reached safe harbor. How could I ever know?

Oh, well, I think, *I was going to die anyway. What'll it hurt to give it one last shot?*

The water running down my face, I shake my head, fleeing from the shadows of my mind and choosing, instead, to think of Liz. I think of the way her eyes glimmer like the moonlit sea, the way her hair falls over her shoulders like the rippling waves of sunset, the way her entire face works together to create the smile I long desperately for with each passing, breathless moment. I think of how, when she laughs, it's like the entire world stops just to listen to her.

And I think of the way her lips feel pressed against mine. And the way her heart beats against mine when we lie together in the back of my van.

I think of it all, every moment, every memory. I think

of her – because if I don't, I'll lose myself. And I let the thought and feel of her flood every corner of my mind and wash away every aching thing. She is the sea and I am the shore, scattered in her depths.

And I'm lost for words to describe this feeling, but it's perfect.

In bed, I text Liz.

ME
You're the best. You know that?

LIZ
I know. LOL JK

ME
LOL Goodnight, Liz.

LIZ
Goodnight, Adam.

I shut off my phone and spread my journal open across my lap. A piece of paper falls out of the back and I stare at it, but don't touch it.

I know every word written on its surface like the back of my hand.

My jaw tenses and I grab the piece of paper and start to tear it up, but stop when it's half ripped. Instead I shove it into the back of my desk drawer and hope I forget about it.

Turning to the blank pages of my journal I scribble, *Adventure starts here: with the choice to depart the Now.*

Goodbye, Now.

18

Monday morning begins with a cigarette and the sunrise. Standing on the roof of the dorms, the smoke in my lungs, the cigarette between my fingers, and the daylight in my eyes, I savor the cool, early morning breeze.

Just then, my phone buzzes and I pull it out to see a text from her.

LIZ
You up?

ME
Yeah.

LIZ
Where are you?

ME
The roof.

LIZ
Of the dorms?

ME
Yeah.

LIZ
OK. I'll be right up. Just a sec.

ME
OK

I smile into the sunrise, excited to see her even though it's been less than 24 hours since I last saw her. Though, I guess it doesn't matter because I guess that's what love does.

A few minutes later, she appears at the top of the ladder and crosses the width of the roof to reach me.

"Good morning," I say as I take her fingers in mine and give a slight bow, kissing the back of her hand. "It's a little early to be awake, don't you think?"

"Says the guy who's already been out here for... how long? An hour?" she says with a wink.

Laughing, I see her eying my cigarette and I offer it to her. "Want a smoke?"

She nods, taking it from my fingers and putting it to her lips, inhaling this time with more care than the last time. A few seconds later, she puffs a cloud of smoke into the morning breeze. "You know, smoking is bad for your health," she says, studying the thing between her fingers.

"That's why I do it," I say with a rebellious smirk.

She rolls her eyes. I sit down on the roof, back pressed against the short, brick wall, legs crossed underneath me and Liz does the same.

"It's beautiful," she says, eyes on the dawn.

"Yeah," I say, but my eyes are fixed on something else.

She takes another puff of my cigarette and looks over at me. "Do you come up here a lot?"

"Yeah. Almost every morning. I like to watch the sunrise. Sometimes I'll come up here at sunset too and watch the light fall behind the city." I pull a piece of gravel from the palm of my hand and scowl at the imprint left in my skin, flicking the pebble away from me.

We sit here for a while, admiring the morning.

"So many people miss out on beauty like this because they're too busy doing *things* and racing through life without actually stopping for a second and just *living* life. I don't want to be one of those people. So I come up here and watch the sun do its thing. It reminds me to slow down."

She smiles at me, her hair falling in front of her face. The glimmer of the golden sun on her honey-colored hair is too beautiful to pass up so I dig into my pocket and pull out my phone. I open the camera app and aim the lens at her as she smiles at me. I take the picture, and she makes a face, sticking her tongue out at me, and I take a picture of that too.

"Let me see," she says.

"Nah." I tuck my phone back into my pocket and she scrunches her face up in mock annoyance. Then, dives at me and reaches for my pocket, but I grab her away and we fall onto our backs. After a minute of this, she concedes and rolls away, sitting up.

"Fine. Be that way." She sticks her tongue out at me.

"Okay. I will." I sit up, stretching my legs out in front of me and leaning back on my hands.

Laughing, she looks over at me, finding my eyes and holding them in her gaze. "Tell me a secret," she whispers.

Looking to the sky, I wonder what I should tell her. After a minute, I answer, "I have a tattoo."

She raises an eyebrow, curious. "Really? What is it?"

"It's a moon."

"Cool. Can I see?"

Moving toward her, I roll up the sleeve of my denim jacket. The cold bites into the skin of my arm, but I tolerate it for the moment and extend my arm toward Liz. It's on my forearm, right next to the inside of my elbow.

"Wow. That's really good," she says, the gravel crunching under her as she moves closer.

"I hope so. It was expensive."

She laughs. "Well, it was definitely worth it. Gotta say, I'm jealous."

I suggest, "Hey, we should go get you one."

Smiling, she says. "I'd like that. Does it hurt?"

"It really depends on where you put it. This one didn't hurt so bad."

"Okay, maybe I'll just get one on my arm too. Just to be safe."

I laugh.

"What does it mean?" she asks, her eyes tracing every detail.

"It's a secret."

She cocks an eyebrow, looking up at me. "What? You're not in the mood for sharing?"

I screw up my face for a second, thinking. "Well, I may be inclined to disclose my secret if... you give me another kiss."

She laughs. "You're such a child."

I just smile. Rolling her eyes, she breathes a sigh and leans forward onto her knees. I close my eyes and wait for her lips to reach mine. Instead, though, I feel the warmth of her lips on my forehead and then it's gone.

My eyes pop open. "What was that?"

With a coy grin, she winks and says, "You never said *where* I had to kiss you."

I feign a glare for a second, then sigh, defeated. "Fine," I say, "It's nothing special. I just... thought it looked cool."

She blinks. "That's it? That's the secret?"

Grinning, I offer a shrug.

"Ugh. You're the worst!" She laughs, then asks, "Are you close to your parents?"

Random. But it was bound to come up at some point. "My dad's not really in the picture." I run my fingers through my hair. "But I'm close to my mom. Well, as close as I can be. There's a lot she doesn't know. A lot I don't tell her," I say, chewing the inside of my lip.

"Like?"

"Like my smoking or drinking or that we're traipsing around the world together, just you and me."

"Well, if it makes you feel any better, I can claim partial responsibility for at least one of those secrets."

"It does. Thanks." My mind travels to the story of the straw that broke the camel's back. "Some secrets are meant to be shared, I guess. Even if you don't intend for them to be."

"That's why people exist, after all. If we were meant to be alone then we wouldn't be surrounded by people all the time. People exist so no one has to be alone." She lies down on her back and crosses her arms under her head.

Her words take me by surprise. I've never thought of it that way. If you're alone, it's because you choose to be. The revelation takes my heart by storm and I smile into the sunrise.

"Thank you, Liz," I say.

"For what?"

"For being you."

She laughs. "You're welcome, I guess." Rolling onto my side, I lean across the space between us and give her a kiss.

"You're wise beyond your years."

"Most women are."

"That's sexist."

"So sue me."

I laugh. "You can keep your money. I don't want it."

"Fine! I will." She juts her nose toward the sky defiantly.

Watching her, I whisper, "You're so beautiful.

She blushes and just smiles at me.

"I mean it. You're so, so, so beautiful. And not just the way you look, but every part of you. You're the most beautiful soul I've ever met."

Tears gather beneath her eyes, but I don't give her time to cry. As the last light of the night sky disappears behind us, I take her lips to mine and kiss her deeply.

We part and rest our foreheads against each other. "You make me better," I whisper.

She lifts her hand to my cheek and brushes her fingers across my stubble and she smiles faintly. "We make each other better."

She rests her hand gently on my face and holds it there,

her thumb stroking my cheekbone lightly. We linger there a moment, then kiss.

The world is ours.

19

The morning goes by too quickly – as they usually do. After spending all of it on the roof, Liz and I part with a kiss, each to our own rooms to study.

At my desk, now, I'm overwhelmed by the textbooks and notebooks and assignments. According to my syllabus, I have an essay for *Intro to Philosophy* due tomorrow and I haven't even started. The prompt: choose two world religions and write a one-page essay detailing how they view life after death.

I've got nothing.

I think for a moment. *Does Atheism count?* It would be a bit easier to just talk about Christianity and Atheism, but I don't think Atheism is technically a religion.

Instead, I choose Christianity and Buddhism - one I'm familiar with and the other intrigues me. On my computer, I type my essay title: *Heaven, Hell, and Reincarnation.*

At least it's a start.

For the next five hours, I lose myself in mounds of research articles I found on the internet. I discover that, like Christians, Buddhists believe death is not the end of life. They believe the spirit carries on in search of a new body and the quality of the body in which they are reborn is directly related to their past actions. In other words, *karma*.

It's certainly appealing, I think. But I'm skeptical. What's the point of life after death if you might become a leaf?

After a while, I fall asleep at my desk and am awakened by the sound of me accidentally knocking over my lamp. Sitting up straight, I fix the lamp and see that it's dark out now. It took no time at all for the day to pass me by.

It's Tuesday morning. I've had my cigarette. I've had my coffee. And now I'm next to Liz in *Intro to Philosophy*, my half-baked paper sitting with the rest at the front of the classroom.

Leaning way back in my chair so that it balances on the two back legs, arms folded across my chest, I zone in and out of Professor Garcia's lecture, my thoughts wandering to the girl beside me and the world beyond the walls of the Ed Building.

"'The only true wisdom is in knowing you know nothing.' Who can tell me who said that?" Garcia asks.

Liz is the first to raise her hand.

"Go ahead, Ms. Richards."

"That was Socrates."

"Very good," he says with a nod. He looks to the rest of the class. "Who can tell me what Socrates was saying?"

I raise my hand this time.

"Mr. West," he says, almost surprised. "Go ahead."

"Socrates was saying that when we recognize that we know nothing compared to all the things we can know, we become truly wise. When we assume we know everything, we become fools because someone always knows something we don't."

"Very good!"

Liz smiles at me and I'm the happiest I have ever been.

When class ends, I approach Garcia.

"How are you today, Adam?" he asks as he shoves his laptop and notes into his bag.

"I'm fine. I just..." I don't really know what I'm doing, honestly, and I suddenly feel very awkward.

The professor offers a gentle smile. "I spoke with your counselor," he says. My chest tightens. "He says you've missed several sessions the last couple of weeks. Why is that?"

"I've been busy."

"Doing what?"

I shrug. "Everything."

He raises his eyebrow as if expecting more.

"There's this girl."

"Ah, yes. Ms. Richards, right?"

I nod. "You know how you told me not to be afraid to open up to those who would love me?"

Nodding, "Go on."

I take a deep breath. "The thing is... I don't know how."

Garcia moves around the podium and sits down in one of the chairs. He gestures to the chair across from him and I pull it out, sitting down.

"Why do you feel like you have to keep these things a

secret from the people you care about?"

Thinking for a minute, I shrug. "I guess I just don't want to be a burden to anyone. Jeremiah was the first person I opened up to and he couldn't take it. I don't want to have to go through that again."

"Here's the thing, Adam - if you and Liz really care about each other, none of the things you struggle with, none of the things in your past, none of your regrets or shames, none of that will matter. The fact is that love is reckless by nature. And love *is* blind. - not because it's ignorant to the painful reality, but because it sees that reality and continues to love in spite of it. So, if you and Liz *really* love each other, none of the bad stuff will matter."

Taking a second to think, I then ask, "But where do I start?"

He smiles. "Start at the beginning."

After I leave Garcia's class, I find Liz outside the dorms and ask her if she's hungry. The professor's words churn inside my empty stomach.

"Adam, let's be honest here. I'm always hungry."

"Good. Then, you grab a blanket, I'll grab the food, and we can meet on the field."

We head into our respective dorm rooms and come out a few minutes later. I carry a plate with two tuna sandwiches sliced diagonally, a bag of potato chips, and a liter of orange soda and Liz carries a blanket. We make our way to the center of the field together where she lays the blanket out across the grass. I set the plate at the center of the blanket and we sit down, cross-legged, facing each other. When we finish eating, we lie down and watch the puffy, gray-white clouds.

"What do you want to do later?" she asks. "I really do *not* want to study. I know I should, but... *bleh.*"

I laugh. "Ditto. But it doesn't matter what we do as long as it's three things: 1) wild, 2) not here, and 3) with you."

"I can promise one of those things."

"And I can promise the other two."

We return our attention to the clouds and look for shapes in them.

"Everything feels so simple right now," I say. "And I'm not talking about lunch, or sitting in the middle of this field. I mean life in general, y'know? It's almost like life – right now, with you – feels... quiet. And still."

"Yeah. It does."

"I don't know about you, but it's been a long time since my life has felt simple." A long time. I can't remember a time in my life where everything else wasn't drowned out by the noise and chaos.

Liz sighs. "Me too."

Stomachs filled with tuna, potato chips, and orange soda, we watch the clouds in silence for a while. I can't seem to bring myself to take Professor Garcia's advice.

It's not the time, I convince myself.

Before I can tell myself otherwise, Liz muses aloud, "I want a tattoo."

"Okay," I say. "Let's go."

Walking into the tattoo parlor, the thick odor of cigarette smoke mingled with dry ink invades our senses. Everything about the place is familiar to me from my first visit here months ago, but I can tell the environment takes Liz a little by surprise.

We stand in the small waiting area, just inside the door. Next to the door sits a couple of chairs and in front of us a red-headed woman in her mid-thirties stands behind the counter, doodling in a notebook. When the door closes behind us, she looks up.

"Welcome! Long time, no see, Adam. What can I do you for?"

Leading Liz to the counter, I rest my hands on the surface and lean forward. With a smile, I say, "Hey, Amy. My girlfriend wants a tattoo. Got any good deals for me today?"

She runs her fingers through her hair, scratching at her scalp, her eyes flicking to where Liz stands beside me. "As a matter of fact, we're still running the same deal we were when you came in last time. Thirty dollars for a three inch tat." She stands back and bites her lip, her eyes studying Liz. "Whatcha lookin' for, young lady?"

Liz looks up at me, then back at Amy, brow arched as she thinks. "You know the tattoo you did for Adam? The moon?"

Amy laughs. "How could I forget? It was the most complicated piece I've ever done."

"Well, I think I'd like one like that, but a sun instead."

Nodding, Amy says, "I can do that. Where would you

like it? Same place as Adam's?"

Liz nods, chewing at her fingernail.

As Amy starts sketching a sample in her journal, she smiles up at Liz. "It's real sweet, that you're doing matching tats. You've got yourself a real winner here." She nods toward me and I just smile.

"Yeah. I do," says Liz. I raise an eyebrow at her and she stands on the tip of her toes, giving me a light kiss on the nose.

"I'm the lucky one," I say.

"Sweetie," Amy says, finishing her sketch, "luck ain't got nothin' to do with it." Amy hands the journal to Liz, who examines the sketch.

"It's perfect," she says.

"Great! You want any color or just black ink like Adam's?"

"Black is fine."

"Alright." Amy walks over to her work station and sets the sketch down on a table. "Well, come on over and we'll get started."

Liz looks at me, then moves around the counter to where Amy stands. I walk with her and sit down on the stool next to her.

"I'm sure Adam told you that the forearm is one of the less painful places for a tattoo."

Liz nods.

"Good. It'll sting a little at first, but you'll get used to it."

"Okay. Good." She laughs nervously.

"If you want, you can take off your shirt, or you can just

roll up your sleeve. Whichever you're more comfortable with."

Liz looks over at me. "I think I'll just roll up my sleeve.

Smiling at her, she tucks her fingers under her sleeve and rolls it up until it's up to her shoulder.

My attention turns to Amy as she starts prepping Liz's arm for the procedure. I move my stool so that I'm facing Liz instead of sitting behind her. She smiles up at me and I smile back.

"It'll be fine," I say. "It really doesn't hurt that bad."

"Good."

"Alright," Amy says after a minute, "let's get started."

About an hour later, Liz examines the tattoo on her arm, still red from the needle, smiling when she sees it. "It's perfect!" she squeals.

Grinning, I nod in agreement with all the enthusiasm I can muster.

Liz turns around to face me, resting her hands on my shoulders, and stands on the tips of her toes, pulling my lips to hers.

When we part, I say, "I promised you that this little adventure would be three things – wild, not at the school, and with you. How am I doing so far?"

She smiles up at me, baring her brilliantly white teeth. "You're three for three."

"Good."

Amy clears her throat and pipes up, "As cute as all this is, we need to get a bandage on that tat and you need to pay me."

"Fine, fine," I say with a chuckle.

Liz's eyes meet mine as she rolls her sleeve back up so Amy can bandage the tattoo.

My own tattoo suddenly burns on my arm and I wrap my hand around it, massaging it gently with the tips of my fingers. Now, I feel the burn of the moon on my arm as it reflects the sun on hers. Painted on our skin, this moment will forever be shared between the two of us. And nothing can take that away.

20

On Saturday, Liz and I decide to go ice-skating. Bundled in a grey hoodie, Liz steps into the rink and skates a small figure-eight with surprising ease, carving a neat line in the ice. Meanwhile, I stumble my way across the cold to meet her, grabbing at the railing as my legs shake like a newborn deer. Suddenly, I slip and fall and Liz catches me by the arm, laughing.

Recovering, I laugh nervously, "I guess you could say I just keep falling for you." I hold onto the railing with both hands and try to keep my feet under me.

"You did *not* just say that," she laughs, extending her hand to me. "Here, let me help."

I give her my hand and let go of the rail. She pulls me to her side as we launch ourselves across the ice. Music thrums through the atmosphere and the lights flicker, bright and quick. It's like a disco as we circle the arena, over and over. When the song ends, we leave the rink and walk (well, stumble) over to one of the tables. After removing my skates, I go to the café to get us some hot cocoa.

When I return, handing Liz her drink, she says, "You're a really bad skater."

"Thanks," I laugh. "I try."

"So how do you think you did on your essay for *Intro to Philosophy*?" She sips her cocoa, giving it a gentle blow.

"I'd say it's probably only worthy of a C or a D. But somehow my grades always seem to tell me otherwise. I guess I've always kinda had a knack for barely getting by." I shrug. "You?"

"Eh, it was okay. I chose Islam and Mormonism. That was *fun*." Sarcasm drips from her tongue.

"What did you find out?" I ask, taking a sip of my coffee.

"Mormons are weird."

"To be fair, all religions are weird in their own way."

"True, true." She nods.

For a while we just watch the skaters as they glide past us, smiling and enjoying the moments inside their own little worlds.

"It feels good, doesn't it?" Liz asks. "To feel like you belong with someone, like you're not an outsider."

"Yeah. It does."

My phone is out and in my hands now and I take a picture of Liz as she sits there, her eyes fixed on the skaters, her face telling me all I need to know. Overtaken by a sense of wonder, a thing often found when I watch her, sitting there, living and breathing, I ask, "Want to go to the beach?"

"What?" she asks, a little surprised by the question. She looks at her watch. "It's eight at night."

"So? Just a few days ago we spent the whole night at the beach." I laugh.

"That's true," she laughs. "Fine. Let's do it."

Driving Gus out into the middle of the beach, I park and jump out. I take my shoes and socks off and wander to the edge of the ocean, where the sea loses itself in the loose earth, Liz by my side the whole way.

"Should we?" I ask, staring out at the waves, moonlight bouncing across them as they crash.

"Should we what?"

I nod toward the ocean.

"Why not? What's the worst that could happen? We either catch a cold or get stung by a jellyfish."

I nod. "I'll race you." And then I'm off and in the water before she even has a chance to react. I'm knee-deep by the time she reaches me and we both shiver against the bite of the cold.

"I deeply regret this," she says, teeth chattering.

With a grin, I let the waves lap at my knees for a minute, then walk back to the shore. I strip off my jacket, shirt, and jeans until I'm just standing in my boxers in the freezing cold of the January night. Liz eyes me nervously. I walk back to the water, turn around to face Liz who shivers on the beach, and with a mock salute to Liz, let myself fall backwards into the sea. In an instant, my entire body is submerged beneath the waves. I hold my breath underneath the surface for a minute and just hang there, held up by the currents.

I come back up for air and hear, "Are you crazy?" Wide-eyed, she gives me a look of concern.

"I think so," I say. Then I dive back into the water and

swim out farther. I try to stand up when I'm out a ways and realize my toes can barely touch the sand. I call out to Liz who's still only knee-deep. "Come on! The water's great! I'm numb to it already!" I laugh.

She hesitates, then removes her hoodie and jeans. Shaking her head, laughing nervously to herself, she submerges herself beneath the waves and swims out to meet me. We tread water now, together under the moonlight, among the sea. I take notice of the way the moon illuminates her features. It's remarkable. Her wet hair, though matted against her face, is practically aglow, as brilliantly gold as the stars, and her blue eyes are radiant.

Using my fingers, I pull the loose hair from her face and tuck it behind her ears. I kiss her as we drift along with the current, my feet planted firmly in the sand beneath me.

The moment our lips touch, a spark of electricity passes between us and she pulls away. "It's cold," she whispers and swims back to the shore.

By the time I get back to the shore, she's on her way back to the van. Grabbing my clothes, I run after her. I grab her elbow and turn her around to face me. "What's wrong?" I plead. "Did I do something wrong?" I move around in front of her, hands up, brow furrowed. She stops in her tracks, arms crossed across her chest, and stares down at the sand.

"No!" Her voice is strained – from the cold or from her emotions, I can't tell. "It's just... this is dangerous. You and I, coming out here alone." She looks up at me, eyes darting back and forth. I step a little closer, suddenly so aware of the cold bite in the wind as it presses into my bare skin.

"Why? Why is it dangerous?" I whisper, reaching, but not quite touching her, afraid I might break her.

She doesn't say anything, but I can see the tension building in her eyes.

"Why?" I press.

"Because when I'm with you, it's like I lose myself in you. I become somebody I don't recognize and that scares me. I don't want this-" she chokes, putting her hands on my chest, pushing me away, pulling me in, "I don't want us to break."

"Where's this coming from?" I ask, gently holding her elbows, trying to keep her close to me. I'm shivering, but, for now, I shrug off the cold.

"Everything in me is screaming that we can't do this. That we can't just run off together and do what we want. But when I'm with you, it just... it feels so right. And when I look at you, I feel like I belong somewhere. Finally." She pauses and looks up at me and I see the tears that have formed in her eyes. "But I'm scared. I don't trust myself. I don't trust that I can hold all these parts of me together. I feel like there's something inside me and it's fighting its way out."

"Maybe you should stop fighting it," I whisper. We're close now. Our foreheads are practically touching and I can feel her breath on my lips. "Let go, Liz."

She doesn't say anything as we look at each other, eyes only inches apart. Tears gather under her gaze, but she blinks them back.

She shakes her head. "I can't."

"You can."

And then she kisses me, pulling my body to hers. Her arms wrap around my neck as I wrap mine around her waist. As I kiss her, I can feel myself slipping. I feel the desire as it wrests all control from my grasp.

Somewhere inside this infinity, we slide the door open and stumble into the back of the van. She falls into me as, somehow, we move both slow and fast at the same time. My heart races and her breath is hot across my skin, her lips drawing me in. And we're just two broken people, the two halves of a broken heart desperate for each other, desperate to feel that connection just one more time. Desperate to know what it's like to be alive. Desperate to mend each other and to be mended.

My fingers hook under her shirt and I pull it up and over her head as we lose ourselves in our moment. I'm surrounded by the refrain of the sea, the song of my beating heart, and I think this is what love must sound like: broken hearts dancing on crashing waves.

21

When I wake, Liz is beside me, pressed into me, fast asleep. Under the blanket, my arm wraps around her back and her head rests on my shoulder. Her breaths are shallow and I can feel the warmth across my bare chest.

The Sunday morning chill casts a thick haze over the windows so I can only see the distorted blue of the sea just a few yards away. I hear it, though faintly. It whispers through the closed van doors, soothing me back to sleep.

I wake again a little while later as Liz begins to stir. Dazed, she sits up, wrapping the blanket around herself. I pull myself up to sit next to her.

"Did we...?" she whispers, eyes wide.

"Yeah. We did."

She buries her face in her hands and starts to cry and I don't know what to do. I don't know why she's so upset. So I do the only thing I can think to do. I pull my clothes back on and hand her clothes to her. I step out of the van and let her get dressed. When she's done I open the door and ask, "What's wrong?"

"Just... take me back to school. Please." She's managed to mostly calm herself, but there's something unfamiliar in her eyes and I can't figure out what it is.

I drive her back to school and the cab of the van is utterly silent. Liz keeps her eyes fixed on the world outside the window, her hands folded neatly in her lap, her hair falling down to cover the side of her face.

I can't see her eyes anymore.

I don't know what's happening.

I don't know what I did.

There's a sharp ache in my chest and I clench my teeth, grinding them against each other until my jaw hurts. My hands tense around the steering wheel, knuckles white.

As soon as I park, Liz is out of the van before I even have a chance to unbuckle. I try to follow her, but she disappears into the girl's dorm and I'm left standing outside.

The campus is silent. The air is cold. Everyone's asleep, but Liz and I. Liz is gone, but I'm still here. And I'm alone. And I'm confused.

22

I'm the master of fake smiles. The trick is you have to narrow your eyes a little. Some people think fake smiles don't reach your eyes, but a slight squint will fool them. Most people don't even care to see past fake smiles anyway.

Sitting across from Dr. Keller for so many sessions, I've mastered the art. As he talks to me now, I arm my face with a fake smile. I won't let him know that I'm not okay. I would have skipped our Monday session this week too, except he called me repeatedly and I was tired of screening his calls. Instead, I subjugate myself to an hour of psycho-babble and false hope.

"How are you doing, Adam?" he asks.

"Fine," I say. In a way, I don't even know if it's a lie because I don't know what's going on with Liz. I don't know anything and it's messing with me and I'm not okay because I'm confused.

"I wish you would've let me know that you were going to skip some of our sessions."

"Yeah, well, I was busy participating."

"Participating in what, Adam?" I almost roll my eyes, but I catch myself.

"Life, Dr. Keller."

"And how's that going for you?"

I think of the last six weeks, of meeting Liz, of the adventures, of finally feeling like I belong somewhere, of feeling like I was in control of something for once. And in one night, everything fell apart.

And I don't even get to know why.

"It was fine," I say.

"Just fine?"

"Yeah."

He sits back in his chair and adjusts the glasses on the end of his nose, staring down at his notes. "Adam, you have to learn how to communicate beyond just 'fine.' If you don't, you can't be upset when other people have no idea how to be there for you."

There it is: the blame rests squarely on my shoulders. What Jeremiah said and did? *My fault.* Liz's strange behavior? *My fault.* The chemical imbalance in my brain? *My fault.*

That sounds about right. "Okay," I say.

Crossing my arms over my chest, I stare down at the edge of Dr. Keller's desk. I don't care enough to make eye contact with him – or anyone for that matter. The only eyes I care to see right now are Liz's. And there's nothing I can do about that.

"Where's your head at right now, Adam?"

I think for a moment, pondering the choice between the truth and a lie. But I have no energy for the truth today. "I'm feeling pretty okay, I guess."

"Mm-hmm." He scribbles a note in that maddening

yellow pad and I want to yank it from his desk and burn it, but I resist the urge. "Do you feel in control of yourself?"

I laugh. "I did. Once."

"And what happened that made this a one-time deal?"

"I don't know." And that's the truth.

"What can you do to take back control of your life?"

I can only think of one thing that adequately answers Dr. Keller's question. I picture the Golden Gate Bridge. But not as it was when Liz and I were there. I picture it as it was six weeks ago when it was just me, hanging over the edge, looking down at the waves reaching to swallow me. The sky pressing down on me, urging me to turn back. But now there's nothing for me to turn back to. I've lost my grip on everything and it's all crashing down around me.

"Die," I say.

23

I haven't been home in three days. I haven't seen my parents since it all happened. The image of Dad on the floor, face bleeding because of me flash across the forefront of my mind.

The cold San Francisco night wraps itself around me, biting into me. Breaking me. Sirens roar in the distance and a million strangers walk by, keeping their distance.

Smart.

Pulling the blanket tighter around myself, I close my eyes and exhale. My thoughts all bleed together and I can't separate one from the other.

whathaveidone whohaveibecome howdidigethere

In my mind, I see the anger in Dad's eyes. I see the fear in Mom's. My fist still throbs, bruised and scarred and all I can think is I deserve this. *But I don't know why. All I wanted to do was protect Mom. From him. But I shouldn't have to protect her from him. I shouldn't have to be afraid of him. This isn't how it's supposed to be.*

How can I ever go home? How can I ever face them?

My heart pounds, afraid. Afraid of what he might do to her if I'm not there to stop him. Afraid of what I might do to him if I am. I can't leave her alone.

I have to go back.

24

I skip my *Intro to Philosophy* class Tuesday morning because I don't see any reason to go. I can't bear the empty seats beside me. So instead, I stay in my room all day, drowning the voices inside my head by binging on the first two seasons of *The Walking Dead.*

This is life, I scribble onto one of the half-filled pages of my journal. *You're born and then at some point along the way you die. And it doesn't matter what happens after that, because you're just the walking dead. Existence is all there is. Life isn't real. Love isn't real.*

It's all fake smiles.

The frustration and the confusion and the anger swells inside my gut and I can't take it anymore. I can't take it, the not knowing. I don't deserve this. No one deserves this.

So I grab my phone off my desk and text Liz before I can stop myself.

ME
What's going on? Why are you ignoring me? What did I do?

No response. After five minutes I text her again.

ME
Hello? Liz?

No response.

With a shout, I throw my phone across my room. It lands against the wall with a loud thud and clatters to the floor. Pulling at my hair, I collapse to the ground as silent sobs pulse through my chest. I can't breathe. It's like all the oxygen has been vacuumed out of my room.

In this moment, on the floor of my dorm, I'm shattered. And I wish I could pull myself together, but I'm not that strong. I've never been that strong. Liz was the one person who gave me the strength I needed to face the world.

Now that's gone too.

And the world is too big and too dark for me to face alone.

What do I do?

25

I'm slipping.

I'm drowning in the same ocean that once made me feel so endless, but now I see the end; I see the shadows and the cold in its depths. It's like my stomach is made of lead and it's just dragging me. Deeper and deeper, I go.

I'm drowning. The water fills my lungs so full I feel like they might burst.

This is my life now.

The days are a blur. I think it's been a week since that Sunday. I don't know anymore. I've stopped attending my classes. I've locked myself in my room. But I don't think anyone notices. Because no one knocks. No one calls. No one texts.

At some point I decide to shower. I check my phone and see that it's 10:17AM, Saturday February 13th. I toss it on my bed. Why do I need to know the day or the time or even the year? What does any of it matter? We spend so much of our lives categorizing everything by these numbers and they're all just so... *meaningless*. We do it just to feel like we have a hold on time.

But the thing is, time is a wild, boundless thing and it can never be defined by any one man. Time is the master of man. Man is not the master of time.

I pull my towel from around my waist and hang it on the hook outside the shower stall. I step inside and turn the water on. I don't bother adjusting the temperature. Instead, I let the ice-cold water cascade over my entire body, numbing me, freezing me. I stare up, up, up at the ceiling. Up, up, up into the flickering fluorescent light. Up, up, up until I'm out of gravity's reach and I'm disappearing through the black hole of time and space, leaving this world behind.

It doesn't matter. It never mattered.

A shiver. But as I stand under the freezing water, I grow used to it. Isn't that usually the way it goes? After a while, the numbness just... becomes normal. It becomes right.

I think I was right to believe that people like me don't get to live life. We only get to exist.

I think I was right when I told Professor Garcia that I'm a hurricane and I destroy everyone around me. But at least before, I knew what I did; I was either too much of a burden, or I was too moody, or I was too challenging, or I was too quiet. I was never meant to be good enough. Good enough isn't good enough anymore.

And that's what I became. The guy who could never be good enough, the guy too broken to be loved.

People like me get left behind and forgotten and abandoned and we're never worth an explanation. People leave us behind and don't bother to tell us why and we end up living our lives wondering what we did wrong, waiting for closure. But we don't get closure.

We don't deserve it.

We get to exist. We're participators, spectators.
For us, there's nothing more.

26

On Saturday I make the four-hour drive to Lake Tahoe because I need to get away from those people, from that school, from the isolation of my dorm. The mountain road is rough and aimless as Gus works overtime to bring me higher. Snow still blankets the mountain and the cold wind buffets against us. When I come to one of the turnout spaces on the side of the road, I pull over and get out. Climbing over the small barrier, I start up the mountainside until I come to a small, flat cliff. I lie down in the cold and stare up at the sky, surrounded by dirt and rock and trees.

The sky is a mix of blue and orange, yellow and red as the sun sets behind the mountains. The atmosphere is a masterpiece and I feel lucky that I get behold it. It's funny; when you've experienced such brilliant life, the colors all seem brighter, more brilliant. And now I stand in the afterglow of that experience, but I can't help but wonder when even that will fade.

Long after the sun leaves me, I'm here, watching the elegy of the stars as waves of orange light ripple across the sky. The snow and stone grinds itself against my back, but I don't move. In the middle of the dreary night, unpolluted by synthetic light, the stars are remarkable.

I breathe the mountain air and let it purge my soul. There's something pure about the air up here, untouched by humanity.

I'm angry, suddenly. I'm angry that humanity feels the need to pollute the purity of nature. Wars and technology, greed and selfishness, anger and hate, all seeping into every facet of life. Men kill each other in wars over and over, never learning from history that wars solve nothing. Corporations destroy forests and flood seas with their waste. People look out for themselves and no one else; they do what makes themselves happy, never stopping to think about anyone else's happiness. The world has become *survival of the fittest,* but what will it matter if there's no planet for the survivors? What will happen when there's no one left to give the last survivor a reason to survive?

This is why life has to be more than just survival: because when we spend our entire lives trying just to survive, we don't know how to do anything else. We don't know how to live. There has to be more than just survival. There has to be – otherwise it isn't worth it.

I think of Liz. I thought I'd found my life in her. I thought I'd learned how to live and not just survive. What am I supposed to do now?

I decide to text her. I can't think of anything else. I'm not done with her yet and I hope she isn't done with me yet.

ME
Liz, please. Talk to me. What's going on?

I wait a few minutes, each second bringing new disappointment. The worst is the waiting, the not knowing, the anxiety, the anticipation of what might happen.

Finally, my phone vibrates and I see her text.

LIZ
I just need some time, Adam. Please. Just give me some time.

I don't own time, Liz, I think. *So how can I give it to you?*

I find a Super 8 right along the border between California and Nevada. Down the street is a Hard Rock Café/Casino. I check in and find my room on the second floor.

Once I'm in my room, I toss my suitcase onto the bed and fall onto it. I don't fall asleep. Not right away, anyway.

It's dark in the room so I slide the curtains open and let the moonlight illuminate my space. A full moon tonight, it feels warm and welcoming. All the light in the world is nothing compared to all the light in the universe.

Right now, I would give anything to have lived somewhere in the distant past. Maybe the Renaissance Era. Or maybe the Age of Discovery. I wonder who I could have been if I lived back when there was still so much wonder in the world, when there was still so much to be discovered. I wonder if, maybe, I could have been the one to discover the Americas, or discover electricity, or create the telephone, or build the pyramids, or lead the Israelites out of Egypt. I wonder who I could've been if everything was different. If this world – the one where I'm falling apart – never existed. If the only world I ever knew was a world full of endless possibility, a world full of the wonder of discovery, where everything was magic and mystery.

I miss it, the wonder. Even though I've never tasted that kind of wonder, I miss it. I miss it like an orphan misses the mother he never knew. I miss it like a housecat misses the wild it never wandered.

It's a strange feeling, to miss something you've never known. It feels like remembering, but in reverse; like remembering something that hasn't happened yet.

And I miss Liz. I miss feeling her close to me. I miss feeling her heart beat against mine. I miss feeling like I belong. I miss our adventures together and the wonder of discovering every new and hidden part of her. I miss it all and it hurts. It hurts deeper than I ever thought anything could hurt. It hurts like a knife twisting in my gut. It hurts because I know that it will never be the same – I can never have those moments back. They've been stolen from me. And the worst part is that I don't even know who the thief is that stole her from me.

All I can think is that I'm the thief. I did this to myself. I let someone in who couldn't handle the waves inside of me and I drowned her.

I'm the thief.

I'm a hurricane.

I was wrong to think we could mend each other. The only thing we could ever hope to do was destroy each other.

I destroyed her – somehow – and now she's destroying me with every memory. With every moment she's absent, with every avoided glance, she's destroying me.

Too bright now, the moonlight starts to burn my eyes so I lie down on the hotel bed and allow my mind to carry me up, up, and away into the heart of the universe. Like that night at the San Francisco ballroom when Liz and I swayed together, surrounded by dancers and musicians and filled with the euphoria brought by champagne.

I'm surrounded by the stars and the moon and the sun, but I'm this time I'm alone. Liz is gone. I feel immortal up here, but without her it means nothing.

Without Liz, all I am is existing.

And that's no life for me.

Waking in the middle of the night and unable to go back to sleep, I decided to go take a swim in the outdoor pool. When I see that I'm the only person there, I'm thrilled. I have no interest in being around people right now. So I strip off my clothes and dive into the deep end of the pool in nothing but my boxers.

I'm at home in the water. The pool isn't the ocean, but it's close enough.

Submerging myself, I press my feet against the wall and push myself away from the wall. I glide through the water like Dad taught me as a kid. I practice all the different strokes too; the Breast Stroke, Free Style, the Dolphin Kick and the Butterfly.

Emerging from the water to take a rest, I sit on the steps

of the pool, elbows on my knees, picking at my cuticles.

My hair sticks to my face and the water drips slowly back into the pool. I wipe it away from my eyes and fall backward, my back on the wet concrete deck and my legs dangling in the pool. Staring up at the sky, I lay still for a while.

When my upper body starts to dry, I slide back into the water, but I don't swim. Instead, I just let myself sink until I'm sitting on the bottom of the pool. Fully submerged beneath the surface, I sit, completely still, and open my eyes, numb now to the burn of the chlorine.

I hold my breath as long as I can, which is a long time. I notice every crack in the concrete and count every light fixture on the pool's four walls. I watch the way the water distorts the light and carries its rays in distorted ripples to the bottom of the pool. I observe everything in silence, wrapping my arms around my knees, the moments passing slowly. I give a small exhale and watch the bubbles float to the surface, but I don't breathe it all out. It's a process I learned when I was little that helps swimmers expand their lung capacity.

Acutely aware of every nerve and cell in my body, I feel my lungs expanding inside me right now and I force myself to keep still and stay underwater. I don't want to leave. I don't want to return to a world full of noise. I imagine what it would be like if I just never came back up for air. My mind conjures up every possibility, every outcome and, in all honesty, I could accept any one of them.

I could lose myself to the sea. It would feel right. It would feel endless.

I can't breathe.

But it helps me forget. The burning in my chest helps me forget the aching in my heart. And I forget the pain and the hurt and the regret and the not knowing.

I can't breathe.

I'm swallowed by the water and I don't want to leave. I don't want to go back to a world where I'm alone. I just want to forget. I want to forget what it felt like to be alive. Because if I don't remember what it was like, then I haven't lost anything.

I can't breathe.

So I come up for air.

27

Once I'm back at the school, the days pass by in fragments. I barely go to class and when I do, I'm not really there. I haven't seen Liz in days.

I feel empty.

Numb.

Guilty.

l o s t

An endless cycle of torment, that feeling – that guilt – forces me to keep remembering Liz, every hour of every day. I can't escape the thought of her. She consumes me like the sea consumes the earth. She has brought me to her treacherous depths and I can't escape her.

I see her eyes in the stars and I hear her heartbeat in the wind.

How could I ever forget?

How do I move on from this?

How do I grieve something that was never mine?

28

I knock on the door.

This used to be my home. And now I feel like an unwelcome guest.

A million years pass before the door swings open. Mom stands in front of me and all of the sudden I'm sobbing, shoulders shaking as I look down at her.

She rushes me and pulls me into her arms, holding me tight.

"Adam, I was scared to death," she says through tears.

"I'm sorry, Ma," I choke. "Where's Dad?"

She looks up at me and, voice shaking, says, "The day after you left, he was drinking and he got really upset again." She inhales sharply. "He took the car. There was a wreck." Sobbing again, "Adam, your father died last night."

It's like a tidal wave has crashed into my chest, crushing me, and I fall to the ground, falling backwards against the porch railing.

Mom gets down on the ground beside me, weeping, gripping the sleeves of my shirt.

Whole body trembling, I sob. It all comes crashing in. My whole life evaporates in front of me as I remember my father. The man who taught me to swim, to ride a bike, to skateboard. *The man who watched the clouds with me, played video games with me.*

And I remember my father, the man who started drinking too much. The man who lost his temper too easily. The man who lost himself.

I grieve for them both. I grieve the loss of the man he was. I grieve because the last time he saw me, my fists were drenched in his blood. And I grieve because this is my life now. I'll never be able to turn back time. This is it.

My father's gone. And no one will know him for the man he was when I was young. To everyone else, he died a drunk.

And I'm angry. I'm angry about all of it. But all I can do is sit here in my grief.

And it's much too heavy.

29

The first glimpse of Spring arrives the last week of February. As I walk to class Tuesday morning, the warm breeze brushes across my arms, giving me goosebumps.

For the first time in a long time, I see Liz ahead of me, walking alone. She wears a hoodie that's way too big for her slender frame. It hangs almost to her knees, draped over her black jeans.

I don't see her eyes, though. She doesn't turn around. I can't bring myself to call her name. Instead, I pull my hood tighter around my face. I don't want her to see me. I don't want her to see what I've become.

During class, I watch her out of the corner of my eye the whole time. It feels good just to be able to see her again. I think she must spend most of her free time in her dorm room because as far as I can tell none of the other students hang out with her either.

I can relate.

After class, she disappears and I can't find her so I make my way across the parking lot back to the dorms. I open the door and right in front of me is Jeremiah. We almost run into each other, but stop just short of it. And now we're both standing in front of each other and I can't move. My stomach twists and turns and my mouth opens to speak, but nothing comes out.

I'm frozen, mind spinning, remembering.

Knocking on his door, I wait for him to answer. A lump forms in my throat as I remember what he said about me to Oliver.

But I have to try. I can't let go without at least trying. His friendship was too important to me; it's at least worth the effort.

The door swings open and Jeremiah stares at me. "Adam," he says, surprised.

"Look," I start to say. I've played it over and over in my head. But I've only got one shot to say it. "I'm sorry, okay? I'm sorry that I put my mess on you. I'm sorry that I counted on you for so much. I'm sorry that I've not been a better friend. I'm just... I'm sorry. For everything. I didn't mean to... drain you." I wince. "I've never had a friend before. Not anyone I could trust, anyway. And I guess I just put too much on you all at once."

He blinks, jaw tense. "Seriously, Adam?" He scoffs.

"What?" I furrow my brow, taken aback.

"You always do this. You come and apologize for this stuff, but nothing ever changes! It's the same thing over and over and over again."

I blink, clenching and unclenching my jaw. Angry. Hurt. And a billion other things.

He doesn't stop there. He raises his voice louder and louder and some of our classmates come out of their rooms to see what's going on. "It's like you're trying to manipulate me into feeling sorry for you so you can keep using me to feel better about yourself."

"I never asked you to help me," I growl, jamming my finger in his chest, pushing him back into his room. "I never asked you for anything. You were the one who came to me."

"Because you were sitting outside, cutting yourself. What was I supposed to do?"

"You could've ignored me like everyone else! Instead of letting me trust you and then going behind me back and talking down about me to one of our friends."

"Friends? You think Oliver is your friend? That's funny because you're never there for him when he needs a friend. You want all of us to be there for you when you're going through stuff, but you've never tried to be there for any of us. You always play the victim and I'm sick of it!"

"You know what I've been through," I say through clenched teeth. "I confided in you. I opened myself up to you. All because you told me that it was okay. All because you told me I could trust you, that you would be there for me no matter what. I'm sorry I wasn't a better friend, but at least I was trying. I try every day of my life to be better. For myself. For my family. And, yeah, for my friends. But you? You stopped trying. You stopped caring."

"Because you kept pushing me and pushing me!" he cries, throwing his hands up in the air as if I'm just not getting it. "What did you think would happen? Every time I said the wrong thing you'd go off the deep end. I just can't deal with that anymore. I can't..." he says, shaking his head.

"I can't deal with you anymore."

"I never asked for your help. You're the one who lied."

"Because you were going to kill yourself!" he shouts.

And I punch him.

We're on the ground now, me on top. I punch him again, clipping him under the eye. Before I can throw another punch, he knees me in the side and throws me to the floor. Then he's on me and punches the side of my face.

I hear shouting, but can't make out what anyone is saying. I figure it out when a group of our classmates rushes over to wrestle Jeremiah off of me. They manage to separate us, holding us by the arms so we don't lunge at each other again.

"I'm sorry, okay?" I shout at him, head pounding. I shake myself loose from the guys' grip and walk away, toward my room.

"You need to get help, Adam!" Jeremiah shouts as I slam the door shut behind me.

Jeremiah just stares at me, waiting. For what, I don't know.

"Are you gonna move?" he asks, his tone sharp.

"I- um... sorry." I step to the side, holding the door open.

He rolls his eyes. "Whatever."

And that's it for me. The anger swells inside me, beyond the breaking point. All the months of pain have taken their toll and I feel *everything* surge through every vein in my body, breaking out through every cut in my skin.

"What's your problem?!" I shout as he's walking away.

He turns around slowly. "Excuse me?"

There's no going back now and I couldn't stop the wave of emotion even if I tried. "*You* hurt *me*, remember?" I shout through gritted teeth. "*You* abandoned *me*. It wasn't the other way around. All I did was trust you and believe you when you said you'd be there. I believed in you and you betrayed me." We've been here before. It's all too familiar.

Jeremiah looks stunned and I see the anger slowly creeping into his expression. "I never asked you to unload your problems onto me!" he shouts. "I never told you that I was perfect. I'm a sinner just like you. I'm human. Just like you."

I scoff as the tears burn my eyes, but I don't stop them. "Is that your excuse? You're *just a sinner*? Do you think that makes it okay to break your promises? Do you think that God's going to excuse you for treating people like this? Do you think you just get to live your life, hurting people, and telling them 'Oh, well, I'm just a sinner. Sorry.' Do you? No, you don't! *You* control how you act. *You* control whether or not you keep your promises. *You* control your 'sin'. And *you* made the conscious decision that you were done with me."

"We're all sinners, Ada-"

"Shut up!" I laugh. "You don't get it, do you? You had every capacity to keep your promises, but when things got hard - when I told you that I wanted to kill myself? You acted like it was no big deal and then when I got mad at you for that you ditched me two days later. I was already broken and you crushed me," I seethe. "You acted like what I was going through was just something that I could *get over* and it wasn't because you wanted to see me get better. It was because you didn't want to deal with it anymore."

"You don't know what you're talking about," he mutters.

"Yeah, I do. I've sat back for months watching you live your life as if I never existed. As if I was nothing. But I'm not nothing because I'm still here and I'm still trying to pick up the pieces of me that you left on the floor."

His expression is blank now. "It's not my fault."

"Dear God, would you shut up? Stop making excuses for yourself and own up to it. Maybe then *both of us* can finally move on."

"It's not my fault," he whispers again. He doesn't even look at me. He stares right past me, out at the parking lot. I ignore the people who've begun to gather around us. I don't know if Liz is among them or not, but I can't even think about that right now.

"Stop saying that!" I shout. "All I ever wanted was for you to keep your promises and be there for me – through thick and thin, like you said – but I guess that was asking too much. I guess you were too weak to handle the hard stuff." I feel the disgust burn itself onto my face as I look at him. "You may think I'm weak. You may think I'm nothing. You may think I'm forgettable. And maybe it's true." I point my finger at him, my entire arm trembling with the weight of it all. "But at least I'm not you. At least I don't give up on people when they need me the most."

I turn and leave just as Jeremiah whispers again, "It's not

my fault."

And I hate him for his excuses. I hate him for making me shoulder all this pain on my own.

I hate him.

30

Everything is different.

The days are darker, even though it's nearly Spring. Maybe it's just me.

I don't feel anything anymore.

The pain has turned to numbness. The hurt has become scars on my chest and arms. I let myself bleed, hoping to relieve the pressure building up inside of me.

I barely leave my dorm room anymore. When I do, it's only to go to the roof to smoke.

I don't eat. I don't sleep.

I never see Liz anymore. I gave up texting her a long time ago. I grew tired of reading her last text over and over, every day.

I just need some time, Adam. Please. Just give me some time.

I guess a-month-and-a-half isn't time enough.

Time is a cruel joke.

31

I can feel myself disappearing. Little by little, the fire that burned inside of me turns to ash. With every passing day, another piece of me fades away.

And I can't do anything to stop it.

Sitting cross-legged on the roof of the dorm building, I stare into the distance at the setting sun, my eyes half open, half closed. A cigarette dangles from my fingertips and I lift it to my lips periodically. In my other hand is a half-empty bottle of Corona. I take a sip and ignore the bitter mixture of smoke and beer as it slides down my throat.

I look down at my journal, open in front of me, its pages flapping in the evening breeze. Tears and blood and ink and paper, these are the things I know. These are the things I hold onto. These are the things I cherish. These are the things that define me now.

I open to the very last blank page and pull out the half-torn, folded piece of paper. It feels strange in my hands as I turn it over, inspecting the outside of it before I begin to unfold it. I take another drag of my cigarette and grind my teeth together as I observe each word, my fingers caressing the page as if it were some beautiful thing when, in fact, it's the exact opposite. I'm gentle because I know the danger in each word. I hold it carefully as if it were a grenade and just one wrong move, one wrong touch, could set it off and I would be scattered into oblivion.

I read it and re-read it, over and over until the light is gone and it's just me and the night and the pages of my life.

This is all that's left of me. This is what I've become.

My hands are smeared with black ink and cigarette ash as I grip my pen in one hand and the folded page in the other. I hold onto them as if they are my lifeline.

I suddenly feel out of place, like a fish out of water, here on the school grounds. It feels wrong, somehow.

So I leave, climbing down the ladder, my journal clutched to my chest, and I find Gus among the dozens of other cars. I get inside and turn the key. As soon as his engine roars to life, I shift into reverse and tear out of the parking space.

Driving through the parking lot, I pass the common area, I see her standing there. She's overshadowed by the trees, but I see her. I see her golden hair and her blue eyes blinking in the darkness.

I almost stop, but I don't.

I keep going until I leave the parking lot behind. And I keep going until I leave the school and Jeremiah and Oliver behind. And I keep going until I leave Liz behind.

I don't belong here.

Not anymore.

32

I drive and drive until I don't recognize my surroundings anymore. I'm now as lost in fact as I feel in soul.

Judging by the desert around me I think I must be somewhere in Nevada. It depends on how long I've been driving, though. I don't know what time it was when I left and I don't know what time it is now. It's still dark out, so I at least have some frame of reference.

I keep driving, winding my way through the desert. Growing tired, though, I get off at the next exit. I drive through the back road for a while until I finally come across a motel. After parking, I make my way inside and walk up to the desk clerk to check in.

"Good evening," she says, her voice like burnt coffee – bitter and hard to swallow. "How can I help you?" she drawls.

"I'd like a room."

"How long will you be staying with us?"

"Just for tonight," I say. "I'll be gone by morning."

She grunts. "Twenty-five dollars. Will that be cash or credit?"

I hand her my debit card and as she, very slowly, takes the information and types everything into her computer, I fidget, picking at my fingernails and cuticles until they bleed, biting at the inside of my lip. My heart beats off-rhythm, in strange palpitations.

Finally, she hands me back my card and stands up, turning to the peg board behind her. She looks through the keys that dangle there, searching for the right one. Finding it, she turns around and slips it into my hand.

"You'll be in room 204."

"Thank you," I say.

"Have a nice stay," she says as I turn and make my way to the stairs.

I climb the two flights and travel the musty hallway until I reach room 204. Pushing the key into the lock, I turn the handle. The door swings open and I'm met with the smell of moldy food and dirty bedsheets. I wonder when this room was last cleaned.

Flipping the switch, the light flickers a couple of times before turning on. It's a dull light that doesn't fill the entire space. It casts an eerie orange glow across the grey and black of the motel room. I go to the window and pull back the curtains. All I see is the gas station across the street and the crescent moon that hangs low, kissing the desert hills.

Walking into the bathroom, I turn on the light. Immediately the tiny space is awash in sterile, white light that exposes the dust on the walls and countertop. It's like I'm in a noir film.

Sitting down on the toilet lid, I pull back the tub curtain and turn on the water. Dirt coats the bottom of the tub so I let the water wash it out for a minute. I imagine this room hasn't been used in weeks.

As the tub water warms up, I strip free of all of my clothes and fold them neatly in a pile on the closed toilet lid. I take my phone, wallet, and the half-empty pack of cigarettes out of my pockets and grab my journal and set them on top of my clothes.

Completely stripped of everything now, I stand and watch the water rinse the dirt down the drain. When it's warm, I plug the tub and step inside. I lie back and let the water rise around me. My left hand grips the side of the tub and I lay there for a while, watching as the waterline rises gradually, millimeter by millimeter.

The only sound around me is the tub faucet and the whirring of the motel engineering. It all feels very cold and mechanical, like I'm resting in the arms of a robot.

Drying my hands on the towel next to me, I reach for my journal. I unhook the pen from the spine and open to my last entry.

I'm disappearing. I hope someone remembers me.

I stare at those words and let them sink to my depths.

I feel I've said all that can be said. To Liz, to Oliver, to Jeremiah, to Professor Garcia, to Dr. Keller. And my mom? I'm thankful she's safe now. And maybe she can finally move on and build a whole new life for herself.

There's nothing left to say now. So, instead, I write six little words - six little constellations - on the page after my last entry.

This is where my story ends.

I turn to the last page and pull out the folded up piece

of paper and turn it over in my hands. I don't need to read it again. (If I wanted to, I could recite it by memory.) But I do unfold it and set it on top of my journal. Grabbing my wallet, I open it and remove the familiar object.

I sink back into the tub, my back slouched and my head resting against the tile wall.

I look at the razor that rests treacherously between my forefinger and thumb. It's such a strange, familiar object. It's left its marks all over my body. On my chest, my arms, my wrists, my stomach. With my free hand, my fingers trace every ugly scar. There's a strange pride in knowing that each scar represents a fracture in my life and that I've survived each one. It's a strange euphoria to remember the moments that taught me to let myself bleed. So many people try so hard to bandage their lives and make sure their masks don't slip that they forget to let themselves bleed. They forget to let their humanity show.

I've never been one of those people.

I will never be one of those people.

Never.

I remember it all so clearly now. I remember everything, every face, every breathless moment, every thrill, every adventure, every heartbeat. I remember when Jeremiah took me to coffee. I remember when Oliver and I took a walk through downtown San Francisco and we didn't have to talk because it was enough to just hang out and be friends. I remember when I met Liz and when I didn't want her to sit next to me or introduce herself to me, but she did anyway. I remember when she first spoke in

Intro to Philosophy about seeing bits of heaven in the everyday good things. I remember when we swayed together, surrounded by dancers and music, hearts full of adventure and stomachs full of champagne. I remember when we first kissed as we stood at the end of the world, above everything and everyone.

I remember it all.

And I remember the bad things too. I remember when I overheard Jeremiah talking about me behind my back. I remember when he stopped being there for me. I remember when he gave up and left me to my darkness and my chaos. I remember how it felt when I punched him. I remember when Oliver stopped hanging out with me because he felt like he had to choose between Jeremiah and I. I remember when Liz broke down in the back of my van and I didn't know why. I remember when she stopped texting me and started avoiding me. I remember when she started wearing hoodies and stopped smiling.

I remember it all, the good and the bad. They're the talking heads sitting on my shoulder reminding me every day of my life, never letting me forget – not for a moment.

I could never forget. As much as I want to. It's not in my blood. The memories hurt, though, and they remind me of why I'm here.

And now, surrounded by the water, at home in my pseudo-sea, I lift the blade and examine it under the pale light. It glimmers silver and its razor edge sparkles as though it were made of a billion tiny diamonds.

Inhaling deeply, I take the blade to my left wrist first,

driving it into my flesh, deeper than ever before. It digs and digs and my blood spills and pours into the tub, turning the water a bright red. And with trembling hand, I take the blade to my other wrist and repeat the process, methodically, mindlessly.

I grind my teeth until it's done and I fall back, my body slumping slightly in the water as I grow weaker and weaker with every second that passes.

I feel dizzy and faint and my heart is racing as I sit, submerged in my own blood. I slide so that my ears are underwater and the only part of me still exposed to the air is my face.

I hear a hum in the water and with each passing second it grows louder, clearer. The tub starts to overflow and pour out onto the bathroom floor. My breathing is shallow and short and my body feels limp and time seems to slow to a crawl.

I'm floating, higher and higher, until I reach the stars. I see them, around me, bright gold and brilliant blue. I see her eyes in them, but I can't bring myself to feel happy at the thought of her.

I can't feel anything anymore except the lukewarm water.

There's no pain.

No regret.

No sadness.

No anger.

There's just me and the memories.

Just me and the stars.

Distant. I feel distant, now, floating far far far above the earth.

I close my eyes and let the abyss take me home.

This is where my story ends.

33

I never thought I would find myself here. Though, I don't know what I expected.

Sitting on the roof of the dorms now, one of Adam's cigarettes between my fingers, I stare up at the moon. I half expected to find Adam here too, but I haven't seen him in days. And suddenly, I'm filled with this desire to fly and be away from this world and everything inside me.

Take me to wonderland, I think, the voice inside my head dry and monotone, my eyes flicking to the cigarette. It didn't take me long to get used to the toxic fumes – it's in their nature to be addictive – now I have a pack with me at all times. I hold onto it as though it were an anchor, keeping me tethered to reality. One problem: I want to escape reality.

How can I let go when I'm still holding on?

I try to focus on the good, to think of all the light in the world, all the hope and the little pieces of heaven. But it doesn't work right now. Not like it used to. I try to pray, but my words stumble and fall to the ground like flightless paper airplanes. I don't think God would want to talk to me right now anyway. It's been so long...

I miss the way things used to be. Before... Before

everything happened. I miss LA and my parents, but I remind myself of why I left.

They didn't believe me.

And that helps me.

But I also miss the way things used to be with Adam, when we were carefree and wild. I wonder if I'll ever get that back.

The days run together like the smoke from this cigarette fading into the night all around me: a blurry, indistinguishable mess that, in the end, leaves a bitter taste. It's Wednesday, I think – somewhere in the middle of February, but I'm not sure. Does it really matter, though?

With my free hand, I massage the sun tattoo on my forearm – it's still a little raw, but the memories that hurt the most. I don't know what I'm doing – why I'm up here, why I'm not with Adam, why I walked away, why I'm hurting him. I hate myself, now, for my weakness – it's just...

It hurts.

My mind falls into madness as I remember.

"C'mon, baby girl," he snarls. "I'm just giving you what you want. I know you like the attention."

Screaming, my voice muffled by his palm clamped over my mouth, I can't see anything clearly anymore between the shadows of the man whose body pins me to the bed and the tears that flood my vision. I feel him on me – every part of me – invading me with unwelcome intentions.

I try to call out for help, but I know it's useless. My parents are out – it's just me and my uncle.

It's just me and the monsters in the shadows.
Helplessness overwhelms me and I'm frozen, trapped.
Staring into the shadows, I shut my eyes and wait for it
all to be over.

Back in the present, I let out a cry and throw the cigarette
across the roof. I let myself fall into my hands and sob,
shaking, trembling.

I still feel him sometimes.

I feel his hands in my hair, his lips on my skin, his arms
wrapped tight around me, trapping me, anchoring me to his
lust.

It's not Adam, I remind myself. *Adam is different.* I
finally bring my breathing back under control. *I am
different.*

But... I can't escape the feelings and I can't escape the
memories and I can't escape the pain I feel deep inside my
chest, where my heart was ripped from me and shoved back
into its cage, a bleeding mess.

I'm trapped.

So I light another cigarette and whisper to the moon, to
the stars, to no one in particular... *Take me to wonderland.*

34

I can't breathe.

My chest tightens and my breaths come in short, violent heaves.

No.

My eyes are peeled wide, staring down at the small white and pink contraption between my fingers. My lips fall open and my vision burns as everything around me starts to spin, like I'm caught up in the eye of a hurricane.

Positive.

As the pregnancy test clatters to the tile floor, my body just shuts down and I lean against the stall wall and start to sob, silently, my eyes clamped shut.

My mind starts racing through every possible scenario, option, and outcome.

Do I tell Adam?

How can I have a baby? I'm too young – I'm just a college student, practically a kid myself. I don't even know the first thing about raising a kid. I don't have the money for it. I'm a mess on my own. How am I supposed to take care of a baby? How will I even tell Adam? We haven't even talked in weeks. I can't just throw this on him after blowing him off.

I brought this on myself, I realize. Because of my fear, I pushed Adam away. I hate myself for letting this happen. *God, what do I do?*

35

I can't keep this baby.

Sitting in my room, curled up on the top bunk, my computer is open in front of me. Two days I've spent in my room, skipping class – I have bigger things to worry about right now than trying to get an A in *Philosophy.*

Taking a deep breath, I set my fingers to the keyboard and, not knowing what else to do, I type: *Planned Parenthood.* I click the top result.

The website materializes on the screen in front of me, and I'm suddenly overwhelmed by the thought of it all. *It would be quick. Painless.*

My hand goes to my stomach and I take a deep breath. In. Out. My lungs expand and shrink inside my chest and for a moment I think I can feel it, the baby, growing inside me. That's not the case, though. The baby can't be more than a mass of cells yet.

Even still... I can almost feel *something* inside me. How am I supposed to do this? How am I supposed to terminate the life my own child? *Our* child. How?

I can't keep this baby, I remind myself. *I can't do this alone.* So I write down the phone number for the closest Planned Parenthood location and close my computer, leaning back against the wall. My arms wrapped around my stomach, I drift to sleep and try to forget everything – even if it's just for a minute.

36

It's hard, sometimes, to separate who you are from the things that have happened to you - especially when you don't even know who you are anymore. I thought I knew. I was the girl from Seattle with a tragic past that no one ever knew about. I was the girl who fell in love with the boy who hated normal.

Now, I'm just the girl who fell.

It takes days for me to work up the courage to call Planned Parenthood. By the time I finally do and I'm on with them, it takes me a second to even figure out what to say.

What am I doing?

"Hello?" the lady asks again, impatient.

"Hi, yes," I stammer, take a pause to compose myself, then just come out with it, "I'm pregnant and I can't be."

"Alright, I'll get you on the line with one of our specialists. Please hold."

Now I wait.

Sunday, March 20th, 3:00PM.

That's when my appointment with the specialist is scheduled for. That's the exact time and date that this nightmare will end, when this will all just go away and everything can go back to normal.

In the back of my mind, though, I hear the whispers. *Adam should know. He's the father.* Then, *I can never tell him. He would never forgive me.*

And I don't think I'll ever forgive myself.

37

Tomorrow's the day – the day it all ends.

Tonight, I'm in my room, sitting at my desk. My school books are laid out in front of me, but I can't focus. I have no energy for anything anymore.

Shutting my eyes off to the tears, I toss the cigarettes into the trash and bury my face in my hands. A thousand thoughts race through my mind, but none of them stay long enough to take root. They're fleeting, distant things – an untouchable haze that settles over me until I can't distinguish one distorted shadow from another. I can't see anything clearly anymore.

My mind has descended into madness and my heart is ruled by insanity. There's a storm inside my chest, swallowing me whole. The memories are the wind and the emotions are the waves and they work together to beat me down until there's nothing left of me.

There's nothing left of me.

The seconds drag on and after a while, I wander from my room and out into the common area. It's only the early evening so it's not been dark out for long, but the shadows are enough. I can't see the stars anymore. They're smothered by the San Francisco lights.

Standing beside a tree, the shadows welcome me. The cold finds me, wrapping itself around my arms like shackles as I hear the familiar chug of Gus' engine. Turning my head, I see Adam's van barreling through the parking lot. My heart stops beating inside my chest and I think that time stands still as our eyes meet for just a second, and then he's gone.

Adam... The thought of his name brings a familiar ache to my chest and all I want is to run after him – even though I could never hope to catch him on foot – but I'm stuck. I'm frozen by the memories and I'm frozen by the fear and I'm frozen by the cruelty of life's sick sense of humor.

Even if I could find it in myself to move, it's too late. He's gone.

It's always too late. And it's all my fault.

38

It's 3:30 in the morning when I get the call that Adam tried to kill himself.

And I crumble to the floor of my dorm room, screaming, sobbing, choking. I don't know how long it lasts. At some point I wake my roommate and she asks me what's wrong, but I don't answer. I can't answer. So she just kneels beside me and holds me until I've cried my throat raw.

I clutch my phone to my chest and my breaths come in short, shallow gasps for air. My roommate leaves and returns a few minutes later with Cassidy, our Resident Advisor, who crouches in front of me. She puts her hand on my shoulder and tells me to breathe.

"Deep breaths, Liz." She mimics deep-breathing and I try to follow her. "In, out. In, out. In."

Finally, after a few minutes, I catch my breath, but my vision is still too blurred to see clearly.

"What's wrong? What happened?" Cassidy asks.

I try to process what I know about what's happened. "He's dying. He's at the hospital," I whisper. I almost don't believe it. I try to imagine a world without him, but I can't.

"Who is?" she asks, calm. Too calm. I want to punch her for being so calm when my world is crumbling right in front of her.

"Adam," I choke. My roommate gasps.

"Adam West?"

I give a sharp nod.

I don't believe it.

I can't believe it.

This can't be happening.

This isn't Adam.

This is a mistake.

This is all just a bad dream.

I'm going to wake up any second now and Adam will be there and everything will be fine.

"Alright, let's get you on your feet," Cassidy says.

"I need to go see him," I whisper.

"Where did they take him?" Jessie, my roommate, asks.

"St. John's." I'm finally regaining my composure, but my chest feels heavy and I feel like it might cave in.

"Alright, I'll take you there, okay? I don't think it's a good idea for you to drive right now."

"Why?" I snap, staring at Cassidy as if she's just insulted me.

She blinks. "You just spent the last thirty minutes screaming on the floor. I don't think you're emotionally able to drive yourself to the hospital."

Oh. Right.

"Okay," I say.

Cassidy helps me as I pack my backpack with everything I can think of – a handful of clothes, my phone charger, and Adam's pack of cigarettes. When I think I'm ready, we head out to her car. My mind is so unclear, so unfocused that it takes a long time before I realize that I forgot to buckle up. We sit in silence as she drives me to the hospital. I don't know what I expect. I doubt they'd let me see him if he's even out of the emergency room.

I think of Adam's mom - what she must be going through...

Outside, rain drenches the earth, pelting the car, loud and sharp. This must be what heartbreak sounds like. The roar of the rain.

When we get to the hospital, I tell Cassidy I can find my way inside on my own. With every step I take, my stomach twists, tighter and tighter until all that's left is a great, big ball of anxiety. I feel sick, like I've been kicked in the gut. I don't even know if I can walk, but I keep going. I keep walking toward the reception desk. Because I know this is what Adam would want. He would want me to keep going. He would want me to find his parents. He would want me to be there for him.

I find her in the reception area just before I reach the desk. I almost break down right then and there, but I don't. Adam would want me to be strong for his mom.

When she sees me, she rushes to meet me and pulls me into her arms and I let her. I let her hold me because I know she needs it. And I need it too.

I'm crying again. Softer, this time. Nearly silent. I let the tears fall, but I measure my breathing to keep myself steady. Heartbreak crescendos inside of me, but I can't let it out. Not here. Not now.

When we break away, she looks at me, eyes heavy under the weight of grief.

"I'm so sorry," I say, choking on my grief. "It's all my fault." Sobbing, Mrs. West pulls me into her arms again, stroking my back and letting me cry into her neck. "It's my fault," I cry. So much for being strong. I guess I was never good at that.

"No, it's not," she says, stroking my hair. "It's not your fault."

I don't believe her. I can't believe her. "It's my fault. It's my fault he's here, in this place." I'm losing control again.

Mrs. West stops abruptly and pulls away, looking me right in the eyes, hands holding my face so that I can't look away. She says nothing for a moment. Then, "Adam's not dead, Elizabeth," she reminds me. "He's going to make it. None of this is your fault."

I blink back the tears.

She repeats, "Adam's not dead. As long as he's alive, our hope is alive too."

Everything falls away from me and I collapse into Mrs. West's arms again and just let her hold me. The arms of a mother are a welcome comfort; one that I haven't felt in so, so long.

I wrap my arms around her too and hold her. Because she's hurting too. She needs me just as much as I need her.

So we hold each other there, in the middle of the hospital, and we wait and we hope. And that's all we can do.

39

"Thank you for calling me," I tell her. We're in the waiting room and the sun is just starting to peak through the hospital windows. I lean forward, elbows on my knees, staring down at the dark, blue carpet. My hair falls in front of my face in a tangled, matted mess.

"Of course, Elizabeth. You're very special to Adam. I hope you know that." I look over at her and she offers a gentle smile.

"How did you know how to reach me?"

"When the hospital called me, you were the first person I thought of. So when I got here, I asked for Adam's phone and I called you." She rubs her finger over the place where her wedding ring used to be. There's still a faint tan line there, telling of what used to be.

"Thank you," I say again, smiling as best as I can.

"I'm so glad to finally meet you, Elizabeth. I just wish it were under better circumstances." She looks away, eyes suddenly distant.

"Me too." I lean back, look out the window to see the sun, and blink back fresh tears.

"Will you pray with me, Elizabeth?" Mrs. West asks.

A lump forms in my throat. "It's been so long since I've

prayed. I don't think God even hears me anymore," I say. I don't know why, but there's something about Adam's mom that makes me feel like I can be honest. "After everything I've done, I wonder if He's disappointed in me, if He's angry with me. It used to be that He was the only one who kept me going, when bad things happened in my life. And now, I don't even know if I can bring myself to believe in a God who heals, a God who loves, a God who brings joy, hope, and peace. Because those things seem too impossible, too big for this world." Quiet tears fall from my eyes as I remember the way things used to be when faith was easy.

"Elizabeth," Mrs. West says softly, pivoting in her chair so she can face me fully. She reaches out to me, taking my hands in hers. "God is not disappointed in you. He's not angry with you. It's not in His nature. He loves you and sees you. And not just the good parts. He sees the bad parts too." She fights back tears of her own. "When my husband passed away, I was broken. I was at my lowest and I didn't know how I was going to move forward. But in that season of my life, I sought comfort and refuge in Jesus. It wasn't easy. Not at all. It wasn't easy to believe in God, just like you said. It wasn't easy to let myself feel loved after my husband. But maybe that's the point. Maybe faith isn't supposed to be easy and neither is hope, or love, or joy. Maybe there's supposed to be a pain to it. Maybe faith is supposed to come from broken places because that's when it really begins to mean something. Faith doesn't mean anything until you've stared into the eyes of the devil and are still able to say that

God is good."

I nod, wiping away the tears. My spirit reaches inside of me, desperate to grab onto whatever hope it can find. But still, the doubts come. Still, the fears come. And the anger. And the hurt. And the shame. It all comes at once to remind me that the darkness is still there, hiding behind it all.

"I'm not going to try to tell you that faith makes everything easier. It doesn't." She gives my hands a squeeze. "Faith doesn't always change our circumstances, but it does change who we are in the middle of it all. So will you pray with me, Elizabeth? I know it's illogical and it doesn't make sense, but right now – with Adam – we don't need logic. We don't need sense. We need a miracle. We need a God who does impossible."

I nod because she's right. What good is all the logic in the world if it doesn't heal us? What good is sensibility if it doesn't set us free? In the moments when darkness presses in around us, we don't need reason. We need impossible.

So we pray together, here and now. Not because we have all the answers. Not because we don't have our doubts. We pray because we need something – someone – who's bigger than all of this. Even if it's foolish, we desperately, hopelessly, violently need impossible.

When our prayer, scattered and stilted, comes to an end, we sit up and Mrs. West smiles at me.

"Thank you," she says.

Sniffling, I say, "We should get some sleep. We've been up all night."

She nods and leans back in her chair, closing her eyes.

I drift off soon after.

Eyes fluttering open, my vision is immediately awash with sterile, white light.

When my eyes adjust, I see Mrs. West sitting beside me. Everything comes flooding back to me and I feel suddenly overwhelmed as I remember.

"How's Adam?" I ask, hoarse.

"He's still in the ICU. Adam is alive, but... they say he's comatose," Mrs. West says, giving my hand a squeeze – perhaps more for her sake than for mine.

He's not dead, but he's in a coma. It takes me a while to work up the courage to ask what happened.

Mrs. West says, "The maid found him in a motel tub, bleeding out," she whispers, her lips pursed. "His wrists were..." a choke, "they were cut. She called the police and they rushed him to the hospital. The hospital called me and I got here as soon as possible. That's when I called you."

Sitting up in my chair, brow furrowed, I ask, "How did the maid find him?"

"He left the tub running and it overflowed. She saw the water leaking through to the first floor and found him."

"Can we see him?"

"The nurse will let us know when he's stable enough for visitors," Mrs. West answers. "It may be awhile."

So we wait.

After an eternity, the nurse comes. "He's stable for now. He's still comatose, but if you would like to see him I can take you." She offers an empathetic smile.

All three of us stand to follow her, but the nurse points at me and says, "She can't come."

"She's his girlfriend," Adam's mom protests.

"I'm sorry. Family only."

Mrs. West looks at me. "It's okay," I say. "Go. I'll be fine. Go see your son."

She smiles and gives me a hug and then follows the nurse down the long hallway.

Sitting down, my mind recalls every moment I shared with Adam. It always felt like he was running from something. And now I know what it is. He was running from his own destruction.

Adam, I think. *I'm so sorry.*

40

The next morning, I wake to find that I'd slept in the waiting room chair all through the night. With a yawn, I shift in my seat. My entire body aches from the grief and from sleeping in the waiting room chair. I wish I'd had the presence of mind to grab a blanket on my way to the hospital.

Adam's mom is nowhere to be seen. She must be with Adam.

Burying my face in my hands, I try to control my breathing. I don't understand any of this. I don't understand why Adam is here.

I still don't fully know what happened. The nurses won't tell me anything since I'm not family. The not knowing, not understanding is the worst part.

It's my fault, I think. I walked away and he tried to kill himself. I drove him to it.

I should've seen it. I should've known. But I didn't because I was caught up in my own mess. And he almost died because of me.

The man I love almost died because I couldn't bear to look him in the eye and be reminded of my mess.

And then I realize more deeply now than ever before that I love him and I don't think those words have ever meant so much to me.

But I'm angry and I'm confused and I'm to blame.

It's all my fault.

When Mrs. West returns, she says, "I convinced the nurse to let you in to see him." She blinks away the tears and suddenly I'm scared of what I might see when I get back there.

I almost cry as I stand. "Thank you. Thank you, Mrs. West." I say, squeezing her hand.

"Please, Elizabeth, call me Mary."

"Thank you... Mary," I say. Just as I turn to leave, she stops me. She hands me a journal and says, tears in her eyes, "I think this might have some answers."

I look at the journal, then take it from her. The nurse is there when I turn around and she leads me to Adam's room.

Walking slowly, I wrap my arms around myself. The cold of the hospital interior, with its gray walls, white tile floors, and clean, white sheets, seeps to my bones and I shiver. How can a place so bland and dismal ever be a place of refuge for the ailing? It seems so backwards.

The nurse leaves me at the door to his room and I stand there awhile, staring through the glass panel, reluctant to open it, scared of what I might find once I step inside.

He lies there, completely still, covered by a blanket. Tubes and wires run from machines into his body and I think I might be sick, seeing him brought so low, his entire life dependent, now, on a bunch of machines.

A memory of the boy I knew flashes across my mind.

He was happy, adventurous, wild, crazy, romantic, independent. And now those machines are living his life for him. It isn't fair.

I turn the door knob, slowly, and open it just wide enough for me to slip inside. I see him clearer now as I come closer. I step lightly, as though one wrong move could kill him. His skin is so pale and he seems so light and fragile, like porcelain, and I'm afraid to touch him. Setting the journal on the nightstand, I sit down in the chair beside his bed and study his face. His hair is ruffled, scattered and I reach up and gently brush it to the side so that I can see the rest of his face.

I feel it all again, the regret and the sorrow, deeper than before. It churns in my stomach like a furious sea. I remember how he loved the ocean, how he would let the waves surround his feet while he just stared out at the vastness of it all.

My eyes follow his arms and I see the thick bandages that cover his wrists and my heart aches at the thought of what he did and why he did it. Alone, in the silence of the hospital room, I lose it. I rest my head on the bed beside his shoulder and sob until I have no tears left.

When I lift my head, wiping my nose with my sleeve, I see his journal where I set it on the nightstand. My eyes linger on the cover a moment before I reach over and pick it up. I turn it over in my hands, caressing the leather binding. It's worn and seeing the tattered pages inside, I want to open it. So I do, hoping that I might find some answers.

Tucked between the cover and the first page is a loose piece of paper, wrinkled and torn. I pull it out and study it a minute before I realize what it is.

It's his suicide letter.

As I read, everything within me falls to pieces right here on the hospital floor.

Mom, he writes, *it isn't your fault. You loved me so much and that's more than I could've ever asked for. But there's been something wrong with me for a long time. And I don't know how to fix it. It's like there's this darkness that's lived inside of me. This anger, this fear, this hurt. I've tried so hard to push through it, to move past it, to open up to people. Nothing worked and I don't know what else to do. Every time things start to get a little brighter, something happens that makes everything come crashing down again. I can't do it anymore. I just can't. And I'm so sorry I couldn't protect you from Dad. I'm sorry I wasn't strong enough to fight the hurt. I know it isn't fair of me to do this to you, but this pain I feel is too big. But if you're reading this and I'm not here anymore, know that I don't feel it anymore. I don't feel the pain. I don't feel the hurt. It's all gone. And I can rest knowing that you're safe. And now it's time for you to heal and to be loved again. I love you so much. Adam.*

I'm crying again, the tears falling like a waterfall as I read. Each word is like a cry coming from the deepest parts of his soul and I feel like I've dived deeper than ever. I can almost picture him writing this, struggling to find the words, to articulate the pain that he was feeling. It was a wordless pain; the kind that breaks you. I think of how Adam always strived to make me feel loved, wanted, accepted. I realize that his was the kind of pain that ran so deep that all he could do was try to love others just as deep and hope that somewhere along the way, the depth of his love exceeded the caverns of his hurt. He hurt deeply because he loved deeply.

There's no way around it; love is dangerous. To love is to open yourself up to pain. Adam knew that and he chose to love in spite of that.

I turn the page over and there's a new entry. I know it must be new because it's written in blue ink instead of black.

To the sun: I love you. Always and forever, I love you. Don't ever forget that. And now it's my time to sleep and your time to shine. Love, the moon

I'm a mess as I fold the page and shove it back inside the journal. It takes me a long time before I can bear to read anymore. But when the tears dry and my hands stop trembling, I open the journal and start to read, beginning with the very first word on the very first page. And as I read, I begin to understand. Everything starts to come together like pieces of a puzzle. I understand, now, what happened between Adam and Jeremiah and Oliver. I understand where Adam disappeared to on Monday afternoons. I understand *why* he was always looking for his next big adventure because now I know what he was running from. He was running from himself and in the end, he wasn't fast enough. And all these people – Jeremiah, Oliver, Adam's dad – the things they did just pushed him deeper and deeper into his pain.

I understand it all now. I understand his pain, his shame, his regret. And I'm angry. The madness that boils in the pit of my stomach is something I've never felt before in my entire life. It's new. It's dangerous. Because now that I understand what Jeremiah did and what Oliver did and what *I* did, I can't forgive them. I can't forgive us.

We broke him. And I pray - I *pray* - I get the chance to mend him.

41

I practically live at the hospital now. The only time I leave is to go back to the school to get a change of clothes. I can't be there right now, though. Whenever I see Jeremiah or Oliver, the anger returns and it's something I simply can't bear.

The days pass slowly and Adam doesn't seem to be any closer to waking up. His mom and I rotate through his room. We don't want to leave him alone even for a moment.

As I sit here now, holding his journal, flipping through the used pages and the empty pages, reading each word over and over, I listen to the sound of his breathing. It's shallow and faint, but it's there. His breath has become my anchor – I hold onto it as if it were a lifeline.

Picking up his pen, I let it dangle between my fingers before I set it to the first blank page I find.

You tried to kill yourself this week, I write. *I'm sitting here now, beside you, listening to every breath you take. You don't know how long I've cried in this place – this sterile, cold, healing place. I wish I could express how deeply your pain has wounded me.*

I pause, chewing my lip. The honest words hurt, but it's

a cleansing kind of hurt; like alcohol on an open wound. It burns away the infection inside of me.

You don't know how guilty I feel. I pushed you away and I shouldn't have. I didn't give you a reason. I just pushed you away and I'm sorry. I'm so so so sorry. I made a mistake and now you're here, fighting for your life, kept alive only by wires and tubes and you don't deserve this. You don't deserve any of this.

I try and try to figure out why you had to feel the pain of everything that happened between you and Jeremiah and Oliver and I can't figure it out. I don't understand how they can move on with their lives as if nothing ever happened, as if you never mattered, while you lie here, bearing the weight of the universe.

And I can't lose you. I won't lose you. Don't let the wrong people win. Don't let this cruel, cruel world win. Fight, Adam. You're strong enough. You, the boy who showed me how to live. You, the boy who has a thing for the ocean. You, the boy who feels endless. You have what it takes to fight this. Learn to live again, Adam. Because I can't lose you. I can't. I know I don't deserve you, but I can't lose you. We can't lose you. Please, keep fighting. Fight for your life, the life you could have. Fight for your mom. Fight for me. Adam, please, fight. You're stronger than you know.

I lean back, setting the notebook and pen on the nightstand, wiping the tears away with my sleeve. Eyes to the ceiling, heart poised toward heaven, I pray.

It's hard to not be mad at God, but anger is not what I need.

Impossible is.

42

With each passing day that Adam doesn't wake up, his chances grow slimmer. I know the doctors are getting worried. They try to hide it, but I see their hushed conversations and worried glances. And I know Mary grows more scared with each second. I feel it too, the fear. I'm crushed under the weight of a thousand thoughts. What if he doesn't make it? What about the baby inside me? I feel it growing inside of me with each day that comes and goes. And I grow more and more unsure about my original decision - how can I give up this baby when it might be all I have left of Adam?

But how can I take care of this baby on my own? I try to shove these thoughts aside - they don't matter right now - but the days are long and the hours are cruel.

It's the last day of the month when visitors start to come. Relatives and friends of the family all come and even though no one says it, I know they're coming to say their goodbyes. But I refuse to say goodbye to him. He's still in there and he's still fighting. He's going to find his way back to me - to us. I know he will. He has to.

I stand outside his room as the visitors come and go,

watching them through the window. Then students from our school start to arrive, one by one. People I don't know and people that I know Adam doesn't know. And I'm furious because these people are here acting like they cared about Adam when they never stopped to notice him – never once. I don't think half of them ever even spoke to him.

Fingering my necklace, I watch as my RA stands at his bedside, talking to him. I think these are the first words she's ever said to him. As Cassidy opens the door, I realize my jaw is set and my teeth grind against each other. I try to soften my composure when Cassidy approaches me. She puts a gentle hand on my shoulder and says, "He's gonna pull through."

Smiling, I breathe, "Thank you." I blink back the tears. I guess I'll admit that sometimes the words of a veritable stranger touch your heart in just the right place and give you that last ounce of strength you need to push onward.

Cassidy gives my shoulder a gentle squeeze and walks away.

I stay outside his room, terrified that if I take my eyes off of him, something bad will happen. After a while, though, I have to pee and when I've held it for as long as I can, I leave to find the restroom. When I come back a few minutes later, I see him through the window, sitting in the chair by his bed.

Jeremiah's lips are moving, but I can't hear what he's saying. His face looks tired and worn and his eyes are red, but I'm too stunned by the fact that he dared to even show up here to fully register the look on his face.

Shoving the door open, I march into Adam's room and Jeremiah jumps to his feet, startled.

"What do you think you're doing here?" I demand.

"I just came to-"

"You just came to *what?*" My voice is loud - too loud for a hospital room. I try to take it down an octave and succeed after much difficulty.

"To see how he's doing."

"Why do you care?" I scoff.

"What are you talking about?" he asks, confused. Which only makes me angrier.

Disgusted, I laugh. "He wrote about you, you know," I say, lips drawn tight, nostrils flaring, the scowl searing itself to my expression. "In his journal. He wrote all about how you made all these promises only to break them. About how you betrayed him. You stopped *believing* in him, stopped *caring* about him. Do you even care what it did to him?"

"Look, I should go. I just wanted to see him."

"Fine!" I snarl. "Leave! It's what you're good at, isn't it? Adam looked up to you. He loved you like a brother and what did you do to him?" I point at Adam, lying in the hospital bed. "That. *You* put him there. It's *your* fault he tried to kill himself."

"That's not... true," he breathes, eyes wide, his voice cracking just a little. "I didn't force Adam to cut himself."

"No, but you sure did your best to put the knife in his hands, didn't you?" I'm close to him now, in his face, jabbing my index finger into his chest. I hope he sees the utter contempt I have for him, for what he did. "You *knew* the stuff he was dealing with. You *knew* how alone and worthless and empty he felt and you *abandoned* him to it. *You* left him to *die*. What right do you think you have to be here by his side in this hospital room when you're the one who put him in that bed? Huh?"

Jeremiah doesn't respond. He's a deer in the headlights, which is good enough for me. I don't need his excuses. Just like Adam didn't.

"You live your life as if nothing happened, as if Adam never mattered to you. You get to move on while he's forced to carry the burden of your betrayal on his own. What makes you think that you should get to be happy while the pain that *you* caused eats him alive? Do you think you're some universal anomaly that you don't have to take responsibility for your actions?"

"Look, Adam made his own choices. I'm sorry for what I did, but it's not like I can change the past. What happened, happened." Jeremiah tries to walk around me, but I block his path to the door. He's not getting out of this that easily.

"Yeah, and you made your own choices too. The only difference is that Adam had to bear the consequences of *both* of your choices."

"I'm sorry you feel that way."

I laugh. "No, you're not. You don't care. Not really. You only came here to try and appease your conscience. What? Did you think that sitting at his bedside would free you of your guilt? Do you think it's that easy?"

"That's not why I-"

I raise my hand to silence him. "I don't want to hear it.

You think you're free of him. You think you can just forget that all of this happened. But you will *always* be the guy who broke him. You can *never* escape that."

My entire body trembles – with rage, with disgust, with anguish, with grief. I don't know what else to say. I feel empty now. So I just let Jeremiah leave and I sit down in the chair beside Adam's bed and bury my face in my hands, letting the tears come.

Because, deep down, I know that I wasn't just saying all those things to Jeremiah.

I was saying them to myself too.

I am the girl who broke him.

And I can *never* escape that.

43

Legs crossed, I sit in the corner of his room, the furthest corner from his bed. His journal open in front of me, my palms and fingers are stained with ink.

Two days have passed since Jeremiah was here and I haven't said a word since. I spent yesterday in the waiting room to give Mary some time alone with Adam. It's hard for both of us to see him on that bed. We can never tell whether he's living or dying. It all looks the same from where we stand.

Mary spends a lot of time praying. I think it's the only thing that keeps her grounded. She plays music, too, when she's in the room with Adam. And she sings along softly. I walked in on her once while she was playing "Miracles" by Jesus Culture. I remember the song because we sang it a lot in the church I grew up in down in LA. It's been a long time since I've listened to that kind of music. Maybe too long. To be honest, I don't know where I'm at with all of that, but I can't deny that when I walked in on Adam's mom singing, through tears, there was something there. There was a strength, a fierceness there. And I couldn't help but wonder, as she sang the line *Your life is flowing through my veins*, if it was a battle cry more than anything else.

I admire Mary. She's so strong. Stronger than I am. She's the kind of woman who walks through pain with her head held high, her composure and her faith completely unshaken. I wish I had that kind of strength. Because with every day that passes, I feel like I'm being crushed deeper and deeper into the cold, dark, deep of the ocean.

Adam's journal is the only thing in this world that's keeping me sane right now. I read and re-read everything he wrote and I can almost hear his voice in each word; deep, slightly gravelly in a way that made me think he would be a great indie rock singer, but also warm and gentle as if he knew how powerful words were and didn't want to abuse that.

And I write letters to him too, filling the blank pages with the pieces of my heart that have belonged to him ever since we met. Turning to the blank page where I left off, I set my pen to the paper again.

To the moon: I love you. Don't leave me. I can't do this without you. Come back. Love, the sun.

Just as I finish, the door opens. I stand to see that it's Oliver. We stare at each other a moment before he looks away, glancing at Adam. I don't say anything. My anger has receded, replaced only by a deep emptiness that I can't seem to fill.

"I wanted to come see how he was doing," he says, looking back at me. "I wanted to tell him..." He pauses, searching for the words. "I wasn't a good friend to Adam. I did things... made choices and even though I thought they were the right ones, I think... maybe deep down I knew they were wrong." He stops and turns away from me, taking a step toward Adam. He freezes at the foot of the hospital bed and looks at him, silent for a moment.

With nothing to say, I just watch Oliver closely. I know Adam blamed himself for what happened between him and Oliver. He blamed himself for being so angry when Jeremiah betrayed him. He blamed himself for pushing Oliver away when he tried to come to him. He blamed himself for everything.

"I wasn't a good friend," he repeats. "But Adam was. He didn't talk a lot. Not to me, anyway. We just kind of... *were.* It's like, just being friends and hanging out together was enough for him. He didn't need or want anything from me except to know that I was there."

His tone is heavy, grief and remorse pouring out almost as if he'd held it in for too long.

"I remember, once, we took a walk through downtown San Francisco. We didn't say a word. We just walked through the streets that night. And it was enough just to hang out, you know? Neither of us was after anything from the other. All we needed was to know the other was there." He fingers the footboard, staring straight down. "I guess he was stronger than me. Because I stopped being there and he never did."

He sniffs and rubs his face with his hands, sighing. "I wish I could've been more," he says. "No. I wish I *had* been more."

I know Oliver isn't talking to me or to Adam. It's a release – a release of all the tension that's been stored deep inside, locked away by a world that's too afraid of raw, human noise. Like when I write in the blank spaces of Adam's journal. I understand Oliver. I'm standing in the same place he is. So I let him release it all and I don't dare to steal this moment from him.

"I'll never have another friend like Adam. There was something in the way he looked at you. It's like he knew something – everything – and he understood it all. Like he didn't need you to tell him if something was wrong, he just *knew* and he was there." Oliver shakes his head. "I was stupid. I let a great friend – one of the most loyal friends I've ever head – slip away from me. And for what? Because I thought I had to choose sides between Jeremiah and him?" He scoffs, scratching at the nape of his neck. "There are no sides in life. There are no sides with friends or family or lovers. You either care about someone or you don't. That's it. It only gets complicated when we forget what love is. Love is putting someone else before yourself. It's selfless."

Oliver takes a sharp breath. "Jeremiah was wrong for thinking it was okay to ditch Adam. *I* was wrong. When you love someone and they love you, you don't just get to walk away – not without ruining everything. You fight for them. You fight for them even when it hurts. Because that's what love is." His hand is clamped tight in a fist, his knuckles white, punching at the air. "Adam loved everyone. Even when he hated you, he loved you. Because when you love someone – truly love someone – that love doesn't just go away. It just becomes an open wound. It's still there, but it hurts, and the memory of it hurts." He wipes at his eyes. "Maybe that's why he did it... tried to kill himself. Because he couldn't bear the weight of loving people who stopped loving him back."

I blink. My heart aches at the thought of it all. Adam was a man with so much love to give, and he felt like so little was given back. *No wonder,* I think. I don't think I could bear it either. And then I realize that I *am* bearing it. Every day that passes that Adam is still in that coma, I bear the pain of his absence.

Love is like an open wound. It's ugly, it's painful, and people try to forget it's there. They try to cover it up with hate and anger and bitterness, but it never goes away. And sometimes, they love without ever being loved back for so long that their love turns into something else. It becomes deformed until it no longer looks or sounds or feels like love. It *becomes* the hate that you covered it with. But that love never goes away because even when you think you hate that person who hurt you, you still worry about them. You still hope they never have to go through what you're going through. You still hope they have a good life. You still want to see them happy and successful, even if it hurts you that you aren't there with them.

That is love.

And it isn't the most attractive analogy, but true things rarely come gift-wrapped.

"Adam never deserved this," Oliver whispers, his voice breaking. "He never deserved to be left alone, forgotten and abandoned. How does anyone get by with thinking that's okay? How does anyone justify abandoning someone who would've loved them with all they had?" I see the turmoil in Oliver's eyes, the inability to understand such cruelty – his own cruelty.

My eyes burn as I start to cry with Oliver. His head sags as he weeps, shoulders shaking. I do the only thing I can think to do. I hug him. And we stand there for a while, holding each other, weeping with each other, letting ourselves be broken together. Knowing that neither of us is alone in this, I think it helps us both in our own way.

Recovering, I step back and offer a pathetic smile at him. Eyes red, he smiles back. He turns back to Adam and, pressing his hands to his face, massages the bridge of his nose and takes a deep breath. "If you get through his, Adam, I want you to know how sorry I am. I want you to know that I never meant to hurt you. But I did. And I hope you can forgive me." Letting his hands fall to his sides, he turns, giving me one last glance before leaving Adam and I behind.

Leaning into the corner I had been sitting in only moments earlier, I slide down the wall until I'm on the floor again. I run my fingers through my hair and look at Adam, lying on the bed, unmoving, but still breathing.

I sit there for a while, watching the rise and fall of his chest and I wonder if he hears.

I wonder if he hears the sound of my broken heart.

I wonder if that's enough to bring him home.

44

It's been days since I've said a word, not even to Adam's mom. Where there was once anger, now only a hollow numbness remains. I've lost all energy for anything but wandering the hospital halls while Mary spends time with her son.

I hear things when I wander the hospital hallways. I see things, too. I hear how the doctors don't think Adam's going to pull through. He lost so much blood before they were able to start the transfusion or suture the wounds and his body is weak. I can't bear to touch him because I'm afraid he might shatter. So I watch him instead. Focusing on the rhythmic rise and fall of his chest, I listen to each shallow breath.

I move to the chair to sit beside him. I'm tired and worn and my entire body feels fragile – as if I've become a porcelain doll. My chest and throat are sore from the crying and from the morning sickness as the baby inside me continues to grow.

I haven't lost hope, Adam. It takes me a minute to realize I'm speaking out loud. My voice is cracked and my mouth is dry from the silent days.

"I won't lose hope," I whisper. "You don't get to stop

fighting. You don't get to leave us here alone. Fight, Adam."

My resilience begins to crumble as I cry out, "Fight!"

Suddenly, Adam's body starts to seize and I jump back as the heart monitor starts beeping erratically. I freeze, unsure what to do, then dart out of the room, screaming for the nurse.

A team of doctors and nurses rush into his room and one of them grabs my arm, pulling me out. I hesitate. I can't leave him.

"Miss, you need to let us work," the nurse says.

The sound of the doctors shouting orders and the frantic shuffling of feet and the rapid beeping of the machines swallows me as I watch them work through the door.

Mary comes running up behind me, eyes wide. When she sees, her hand flies to her mouth as she stifles a sob.

I watch, waiting for a sign – anything – waiting for him to pull through.

And then he flat-lines and I'm screaming.

He's dead.

Adam is dead.

45

"We've stabilized him for now, but his body is weak," the doctor tells us. "There's nothing else we can do. It's up to Adam now."

Putting a hand on Mary's shoulder, the doctor gives a gentle squeeze and a reassuring smile, then leaves.

Arms wrapped tight around my chest, I do my best to control each breath. My head falls back and I keep myself from crying because I'm tired of feeling like I'm just sitting here waiting for him to die. There's nothing else I know to do, so I just pray. It's nothing extravagant or anything. It's just me and the God I was taught to believe in.

And I hope that Mary is right and He's not disappointed in me. I hope He can forgive me at least long enough to hear my prayers.

Hope is all I have right now.

46

Mary hasn't slept in days. I see it in her eyes. And I see it in my own reflection every time I go to the bathroom or pass a window. The sleeplessness starts with your eyes, etching lines all around them, slowly pulling them inside your skull, deeper than they're ever meant to be. Then, when it's done with your eyes, it moves to your forehead – there are more lines there now and you look like you've aged a decade. After that, it changes the way you talk. Your words come out like syrup, slowly and all mixed together. Being tired is a lot like being sick – you lose all your energy and motivation and everything becomes a thousand times harder – even the easy things.

I know I need to sleep, but I'm terrified to leave Adam alone. Watching someone you love fight for their life is a nightmare; except it doesn't end when you wake up.

"Fight, Adam," I whisper for the hundredth time, hoping my words somehow reach the deepest parts of his spirit.

I watch him closely. His face is sunken and his eyelids twitch. My hand is on his arm and I stroke his skin gently with my thumb. I crave him. I crave him in the deepest way possible, longing to feel his fingers as they brush against my skin, longing for his lips against mine, longing for the beat of his heart.

"Adam, you showed me what it looks like to be alive." I stand. "And if you let me, I'll show you too." I bend over him and slowly, carefully, press my lips against his forehead. Quietly, slowly the tears flood my eyes again and begin to spill over. I let them fall because I don't have the strength to hold them in.

Pulling back, I see that Adam is still asleep. I don't know what I expected. I guess I thought my touch would be enough. It isn't, though. So I turn to leave because I can't bear to be here anymore. I can't bear to watch the life fade from his bones.

I can't bear it.

Just as my fingers touch the door handle, I notice his breathing is deeper now, faster. Terrified he's about to flat-line again, I spin around. And then I see it. His mouth opens and he takes a deep breath, sucking the air out of the room. I step closer, eyes wide. "Adam?" I rest my hand on his arm and look down at him. His eyes twitch and flutter open and there they are, those chocolate eyes.

I'm laughing now and I'm smiling and I'm crying. At first, Adam's eyes are fixed on the ceiling, but then he looks at me. His expression appears confused and surprised and lost, but he's alive. He's awake.

"Mary!" I cry, my voice breaking. "Mary! He's awake! Adam's awake!" She races into the room to my side, followed immediately by a nurse.

I want to hold him, but knowing how frail his body must

be, I refrain. He tries to say something, but can't form the words.

"Don't try to speak, Adam," the nurse says, checking his vitals. "Give your body some time to catch up with itself."

"I'll let you rest and I'll be back later, okay?" I tell him. I don't want to, but I know I should leave and let his mom spend some time with him. He gives a weak nod and I smile and then leave.

A strange euphoric feeling overwhelms me and I step inside the first room I see after leaving Adam behind, which happens to be a janitor's closet, and as I slide down the door to the floor I feel everything burst inside of me and I just cry. But it's different now. These tears are no longer tears of sorrow or defeat or hope or anger or regret. They're tears of joy and relief and gratitude.

And I feel like I'm soaring right now.

Because Adam's alive.

47

As overjoyed as I am, reality begins to settle in. Adam is alive and it's wonderful and it's a bona fide miracle. But the mess of reality isn't gone. Everything that happened between us isn't gone. Everything that happened with Jeremiah and Oliver isn't gone. It's still there. Reality is just salt in the wound.

And now that Adam's alive, I remember all the things I'm going to have to come to terms with. It's time for me to face reality. The pain is still there. It doesn't just disappear and it can't be ignored. The pain of what Adam did, what I did, and the decisions we have to make.

But I have renewed determination now. Because now that Adam is alive and recovering, I don't feel so alone in it anymore. And I don't feel so scared of my pain. It's like something is unlocking deep inside of me. I'm realizing that pain is a part of you and that's not a bad thing. It builds you into something big enough to hold a universe full of light. It burns at first, but then you start to realize that all that pain was really just lighting your way deeper through the darkness until, eventually, all that's left is light.

In a way, I'm proud of my pain. It's not that I would want to endure it again; but I'm thankful for it. I'm thankful for who it's making me into. Someone stronger. Someone who doesn't run, who isn't afraid.

Reality is painful. But sometimes, if you look long and hard, there's a purpose hiding behind all that pain.

48

Adam hasn't said a word since he woke up. Mostly, he just sleeps and eats. The color is finally starting to return to his skin, but there's something in his eyes when he looks at me and I don't know what it is. It's this blankness – a numbness – lurking just beneath the surface.

I feel lost and I don't know what to do so mostly, when Mary isn't with him, I just sit in the chair beside him while he sleeps and sometimes when he's awake. But staring at him when he's awake seems strange so I try to keep myself busy with my phone or a magazine.

Finally, it comes from out of the blue one lonely April afternoon. Adam speaks for the first time and I look up at him, trying my best to hold myself steady.

"Why are you here?" he asks, voice raw.

I'm a little surprised by the question. "What?"

He says it again slowly this time. "Why are you here?"

"That's a stupid question."

"No, it isn't. We haven't said a word to each other in what? Two months?"

"Sixty-five-and-a-half days," I mutter.

"So why are you here?"

Untucking my legs from under me, I reach for his

journal on the nightstand. "Let me show you something." I fold the journal open on my lap. "I know I shouldn't have, but... I read your journal."

A look of hot anger flashes like lightning through his eyes, but I keep going before he has the chance to protest.

"I was confused and lost and tired of waiting for you to wake up and I had to know. So I read your journal and when I did it was like you were here and you were telling me every ugly, messed up, secret part of you and it helped me because it answered the questions that were burning inside of me. Please know that I only did it because I didn't know what else I *could* do. You were in a coma, for God's sake."

The expression on his face softens, but he keeps silent, waiting for more.

I find the page with my first journal entry and I hand it to him. I watch as he reads, page after page and something in his eyes changes as everything I wrote just suddenly clicks inside of him. He's crying softly, each word awakening something.

Afraid that if I move the moment might be ruined, I stay completely still. And I just watch him, my hands folded neatly in my lap, chewing the inside of my lip.

When he finishes, he cries harder and he's sobbing now and then I start crying too. Standing, I move over to him and sit down across from him on the bed. Leaning forward, I take his face in my hands and rest my forehead against his. For a while, we just sit there, pressed against each other, as everything that happened these last few months – the good and the bad; the beautiful and the ugly – crashes into us.

Through tears, I whisper, "I'm here, Adam. And I'm not going anywhere. Never again. I love you."

He is my everything – my healing and my wound. He is the thing that keeps me up at night and the thing that gives me purpose. And I know that everything between us isn't completely better. Not yet. Life doesn't work on fast-forward.

But he's alive and we're together.

And that's enough.

PART 3

49

Ten days.

Two-hundred-and-forty hours.

Countless seconds have passed since my waking. I've heard stories of people who were subconsciously aware while comatose – others where they went to heaven or hell and met God or family members or friends and stuff like that.

Not me, though.

I never expected to wake up. I never expected to see Liz's face again. I never expected any of this. I thought I would die and it would be over. The last thing I remember was the blood and the sting of the wounds on my wrist and the feeling that all this weight had finally lifted. But now I'm here, alive, and everything is like it was before, but different... in a way.

Mom doesn't leave me alone for too long. I'm in the mental ward, now. I'm on suicide watch. The nurses' eyes burn into the back of my neck when I'm not looking. Under their constant watch, I'm suffocating.

Liz is gone right now and Mom is too. So I'm alone for now.

I stare down at the bandages wrapped tight around my wrist. I want them gone. I want to see. I *need* to see the damage I did. I need to see the wound to make it real because right now I'm floating. I feel distant and numb to everything and everyone around me.

When Liz visits me, I never know what to say so mostly we sit with each other in silence. She still wears her baggy hoodie, which makes it worse because she used to be the most colorful person I'd ever known.

And I've destroyed her.

I hate myself.

I hate myself for trying to kill myself and not succeeding because now I have to look Mom in the eye and when I do I can see that she knows things now that I never wanted her to know. It hurts to know that you've caused someone else pain. And it *should* hurt. The sad truth is that not everyone cares if they hurt anyone else. Either that or they're just too stupid to realize the damage they've done.

I pull my journal from the nightstand and open it up to where Liz first started writing. I trace the delicate scrawl of her penmanship, a stark contrast to my heavy-handed scribblings. There is a heaviness in her words, a longing, but none of it seems to answer the one question I have: why does she even care?

I can't ignore the way my hurricane life has affected her. *I* brought her into this messed up world of mine. *I'm* the reason for her grief. *I'm* the reason she's missed too many classes to allow her to pass this semester. *I'm* the reason she can't move on. Because *I* couldn't manage one simple task: to kill myself.

Wouldn't it just be easier to die? The people I love could finally move on and I could too. I could finally stop this, the pain of remembering, of loving too much.

Liz's words tell me how she loves me and how she cares, but they don't explain why. They don't explain why she spent countless days by my bedside after avoiding me for two months. I want to ask her, but talking to her now is a foreign thing. And now I'm vulnerable, all my secrets laid bare before everyone I've ever known. I've spent so long carefully constructing those secrets around me like a castle wall. Every shadow place, every faded corner strategically placed became my defense. Every guarded weakness became my strength. What am I supposed to do now that the secrets have gone and the shadows have vanished?

My jaw tenses and my teeth grind against each other when the nurse walks up to me and hands me a little paper cup with multiple pills inside.

"What are those?" I ask.

"Medicine," she says. Her face is straight, unmoved, stern. Her eyes are alert and seem to say that if I don't take the pills she'll force them down my throat. She's not a big woman, but she sure is intimidating.

Lifting the cup to my lips, I tip my head back and swallow.

"Open," she says. I obey and she checks to ensure, I assume, that I've not hidden any of the pills under my tongue. "Good," she says when she's done, taking the paper cup from my hands. Then she hands me a folded up page. "I found this under the bed in your old room. Somebody must've left it for you." With that, she walks away and I'm left alone with the thoughts in my head, the medicine in my system, and the page between my fingers.

50

Balancing the page between my fingers, I'm terrified of what might be inside. I don't know who the letter is from, but my stomach twists itself into knots every time I think about it. The not knowing is killing me, though. But the knowing could could kill me too.

After a while, the curiosity is maddening and I can't help it, so I unfold the letter, slowly as if it were a fragile gift.

Once open, my eyes fall on the first line.

Adam,

I'm not good with words. But, I guess, you know that. (I spent longer than I'd like to admit trying to write this letter.) You knew a lot and, I'll admit, I always thought that made you special because how many people really take the time out to understand and learn about their friends in such a short amount of time?

You were always a wallflower and that was always hard for me because you would be on the outside of everything while I was on the inside and I always thought that it was just because you were shy and sad. But the truth is, I was wrong to think that being a wallflower was some sort of disorder I had to help you overcome. In fact, it's the furthest thing from a character flaw because, unlike the rest of us, you took the time to just stay quiet and watch other people. You saw things and you understood them when no one else did.

I didn't understand it, Adam. And I blamed that on you. The truth is that you didn't drain me – I drained myself because I thought I had to fix you. But you were never broken. For all your pain and for everything you've been through, it was a part of you in the best kind of way. All that hurt you've carried – and I know it was so, so heavy – it's made you into the kind of person who loves deeply. Too deeply for shallow people. You know what it feels like to hurt, to ache, to need and you never wanted that for anyone else. And it was like I was caught in the middle of this war you waged with yourself between the hurt you carried and the love you gave and I just didn't know what to do. And you know that I hate feeling trapped, so I ran. I told you I'd always be there for you, but I guess you were right. I'm a liar. I'm a coward too, because I did the easy thing. And I ended up hurting someone that I really cared about and for that I am so sorry.

But please know that I never stopped caring about you; even though I did a really bad job at it. I'm the one who told the dean about what you've been going through. I did it because I wanted you to get the help that you needed – the help I could never give you.

I know you probably hate me and you have every reason to, but the thing is, we have to let go of our hate. It'll only rot us from the inside out. That's why I'm writing this, because I want you to let go of me and what I did. Not for my sake, but for yours. What I did, it isn't your fault and you shouldn't have to carry that around. Let that be my burden.

Move on, Adam. Learn to live again. Find whatever it is that makes you come alive and hold onto that and don't you ever let go.

Goodbye, Adam.

J.

My eyes hold onto that last letter - *J.* I don't need to think about who it is - I already know.

My vision blurs as my eyes well with tears, but not of grief or loss. For once, they're tears of relief because it's like this heaviness has lifted off me. For all that's happened between us, Jeremiah gave me what I needed to let go. I don't need to hold on anymore.

I know the hurt won't go away overnight, but there's something about what he said - that the hurt is a part of me - that renews me. This whole time, I thought the hurt, the mistakes, the stuff going on in my head was destroying me.

But maybe it was just shaping me.

51

It's a strange and uncomfortable feeling to know that you're constantly being watched. By the nurses, your parents, and your girlfriend. (Ex-girlfriend? I'm still unsure where we stand.)

With Liz, as Jeremiah's letter lingers in the back of my mind, I'm tired of being unsure.

She visits me today and we just sit in my room together, reading our respective magazines. It takes me awhile to work up the courage. Finally, with a sigh, I realize I literally have nothing to lose. (Except her. But I don't know if I even have her, so that negates the entire scenario.) "Why are you here?"

She looks up at me, brow raised. She points at my journal. "I thought we went over this already, Adam."

"The journal doesn't answer my question. Not really. Why are you here? Now? You left me for two months without a word and now you're back. It doesn't make any sense."

She sighs. "When we..." she looks at me as if she wants my permission to not say it, so I nod, pretty sure I know what she's referring to. "I was raised in a Christian home where purity and virginity were *everything.* As a young Christian girl it was my responsibility to never compromise myself and save myself for marriage. And when my uncle took that from me..." She doesn't finish her thought, but looks at me, tears forming in her eyes. "I lost myself in you that night. I loved you Adam. I still love you, but I couldn't control myself. It was like... I had to have you and nothing else mattered. Everything else faded away and it was just us, together, in that moment." She wipes her nose on her sleeve. "And after, when it was over, I realized what we had done and I felt so ashamed, dirty. And I remembered what it felt like when my uncle would..." she doesn't say it and I don't make her. "I couldn't escape the shame and I started to blame myself for what happened with my uncle, for what happened with us.

"And I guess," she sighs deeply, "I was afraid. I was afraid that if I stayed with you, I would just keep losing myself in you and you would get tired of me and throw me away like my uncle did. So I walked away. Even though I loved you, I walked away because I was afraid. I walked away from you before you had the chance to walk away from me." She sobs into her hands. "I know I was wrong, now. I didn't realize how much I had hurt you and I hate myself for it." She looks up at me. "I thank God every day that you're alive because I love you. I love you so much, Adam."

Within her quiet sobs, I hear the sound of my own heart breaking for her and I scoot to the edge of the bed. My body is weak, but with every ounce of strength I have left, I reach out to her and press my fingers against her chin, lifting her head until her eyes meet mine. I see the ocean in her eyes. She is everything I've ever wanted. She is my sun, my heaven on earth. She is the adventure I embark on every day and I feel it now, the pain of her choices. I'm not mad at her. I'm mad at myself for ever letting her think that I would *ever* treat her like her uncle treated her. "I love you too, Liz," I whisper. "More than anything. And I'm sorry for all of this. I'm sorry for bringing you into my mess."

She smiles up at me. "I guess our gravitational pull was too strong."

I laugh. "I think we've definitely made a few waves." Then I kiss her, slow and sweet, drawing her every breath into my lungs until our hearts are mended to each other again.

The pain isn't gone. It never will be. But hope – like the light of a thousand stars being born at once – explodes inside of me.

52

I'm kept under watch for another week before they let me go. My only company is Mom and Liz, which is fine by me. Though, I wish Mom didn't have to see me this way. Because now I have to live with the fact that she's never going to stop watching me, waiting for some giveaway that I might be suicidal again.

The sad truth is that I miss my secrets. Except, it seems, with Liz. She's the only person I don't feel uncomfortable around, despite the fact that she read my journal. I guess that's another thing love does; it breaks down all of your walls in just the right places to let someone else get through.

Packing now, I place all my belongings in my backpack, gently as if they're fragile things. I swing my backpack over my shoulder and turn to see Liz standing in the doorway of my hospital room. I smile at her.

"You ready to go?" she asks.

"I've never been more ready for anything in my entire life." I walk to her, putting my arm around her shoulders, pulling her close, and we walk out together.

I stand in the middle of my dorm room for what will be the last time. Everything I own is condensed into a stack of totes, boxes, and suitcases. It doesn't bother me, really. Leaving, that is. I never really felt like I belonged here or fit in with anyone and no one ever paid me any attention. I imagine nobody will notice I'm even gone except - maybe - Professor Garcia who was among those to visit me while I was in my coma. Or so I'm told. I haven't seen him since and I feel bad leaving like this without saying a word to him. So I make a mental note to go see him in his office before I leave.

All the things that have happened since my botched suicide attempt have been unexpected in many ways. At the top of the list is the fact that Jeremiah visited me while I was in my coma and left behind a letter. Behind that is the fact that apparently attempting suicide is against school policy, so now I'm suspended for the rest of the semester. Of course, they didn't directly say I was suspended. They were very careful to sound sympathetic so, instead, they said, "We believe it would be best if you took the rest of the semester off to find the help you need to fulfill all that this school asks of its students."

So here I am, packing up and leaving. Mom wanted me to stay with her until I can find my own place, but I didn't want to leave Liz and move two hours away from her so I told her I would just sleep in my van for a while until I can get a job and buy my own place. She was reluctant - *extremely* reluctant - but since I'm already living on my own and am technically an adult I push the point. For all our sakes.

I'd feel suffocated if I went back home to live with Mom. Not that I don't love her - I do. I just need to move on with my life and I feel like going back to live at home again would be a step backwards. I'm all about moving forward right now.

I carry my things out to the common area where Liz meets me and helps me load everything into Gus' trunk. A few people linger in the common area,avoiding us and I roll my eyes at Liz.

"What?" she asks, puzzled.

"Don't you notice the fact that absolutely no one is looking at us?"

"So?"

"C'mon, no one's that oblivious."

She laughs. "Who cares?"

"Apparently they do." I say, tongue in cheek.

"Well, *they* don't matter," she says, walking up to me. "But I do. And you do. And that's enough." She smiles up at me, her hands holding my elbows as I wrap my arms around her middle.

"Come here," I say with a grin. I pull her to me and give her a big kiss. Pulling back, serious now, I whisper, "I'm sorry."

"For what?"

"For doing what I did. For putting you through that." I lift her hand to my lips and kiss it lightly. "I promise that I'll never leave you like that again. Whatever it takes, I'm yours forever. I'll fight through everything. For you."

She kisses me, lips smiling against mine, then pulls away. "Go double check your room and make sure you didn't forget anything."

"Where would I be without you?" With a wink, I turn

back to the men's dorms.

She just smiles.

It turns out that I did forget a sock under my bed so it's a good thing I went back in. I walk across the dorm floor and stop when my eyes come to the nameplate on the door of the room right next to the entryway.

Jeremiah Jackson.

I breathe, slow and steady, in out in out in out. I wish it was easy to forget, but I know that a day won't go by when I won't think about everything that happened between us. Those things just don't disappear.

As I pass his door, I stop in my tracks and let my eyes trace the letters of his name, contemplating whether or not I have anything left to say to him. I let myself recall everything that still lingers between us, but it's different now. It doesn't hurt like it used to. Because I'm beginning to realize that people like me are born for this. We're born to bear the pain of broken relationships. We're meant to remember every tragic moment for the rest of our lives, even when the other person seems to forget and move on so easily. We bear the pain so they don't have to. We bear the memories so they can let go and move on and be happy. We suffer so they don't have to. We bear it all so they don't have to.

We are built for this.

I am built for this.

Taking a deep breath, the oxygen strengthens my resolve. *I am built for this.*

While I was in the hospital, Liz wrote in my journal that

you never truly stop loving someone if you ever truly loved them to begin with. So I can't help but feel like there's still a love there. Our friendship may be over and that closeness may be gone, but I still hope the best for him. I hope he moves past all of this too.

And that's when it hits me – it's over.

All of this – every broken part – is over now.

I can move on.

53

"That took you forever," Liz says as I step outside the dorms. She looks down at my hand as I'm holding the sock in it.

"It's a good thing I sent you back in, isn't it," she says with a coy smile.

I laugh. "It sure is. One should never doubt a woman's intuition.

"That would be wise." She grins. "Are you ready?" she asks, wrapping her arms around me.

I look down at her. "Yeah. I am." I pull her to me and kiss her gently, our lips touching just enough for the electricity to pass between us.

She pulls away and looks up at me, searching my eyes. "Adam... There's something I need to tell you."

She takes my hand in hers and leads me down the sidewalk toward the field. We follow the path as far away from the school as we can get until we're shielded by the trees. She turns to face me, eyes meeting mine.

"I wasn't completely truthful," she says and my heart plummets. There's no anticipating what she says next. I have no idea where she's at or what she's trying to say or why she kept whatever it is from me. "There's another reason I avoided you for so long. Something else happened." Her face scrunches up as if she doesn't really know what she's saying – at least, not the weight of it. "I'm pregnant."

With that, everything else falls away. My mouth hangs open and for the longest time, I say nothing. I don't know what to say. I don't know what to do. So I say the first thing that pops into my head, which, in most cases, is a bad idea. "Okay."

"Okay?" She furrows her brow, staring up at me.

I nod. "Okay." I say it firmer now, like I believe it. "Liz, it's no secret that I'm in love with you. I've spent every second of these last four months loving you. Nothing is going to change that. Our situation may have changed, but my love for you will *never* change. Whatever hurricane comes our way, Liz, *I love you.*"

She smiles softly, relieved. "I love you too." Then we kiss and it's like the heavens opened over us and the stars are singing their song just for us. (But that might just be my medication talking.)

She pulls away, then, and says, "What do we do, now?"

I look down at her stomach, shrouded by an oversized hoodie. I set my hands gently on both sides and I feel the subtle roundness of it. It's not very noticeable yet, but it's there. And now I know why she wears the hoodie and I suddenly really hate that hoodie. (Even more than I did before.) "Don't wear this hoodie anymore," I say. "At least, not if you're just wearing it to hide our baby."

Her brow furrows and she parts her lips to speak, but says nothing.

"You – *we* – have nothing to be ashamed of. Whether

what we did was a mistake or not, it happened and now we have this amazing new life that we get to welcome into this world, but I will not let my son or daughter grow up believing that I let anyone make their mother feel ashamed of her life. There is life inside of you, Liz. Don't hide it."

I kiss her again, knowing to the deepest parts of me that we have nothing to be ashamed of.

54

As we follow the path back to the school, something swells inside my heart and I recognize this feeling immediately. It's the same feeling I had when I first met Liz. It's the same feeling I had when we went to Point Reyes and the Grand Canyon and Yosemite. The wanderlust has returned and it's insatiable. "Let's go," I say.

"Where?"

"On an adventure." There's something in me right now that needs to purge the bad from my system. It used to be that all I could think about was the past, but now – all of the sudden – the only thing I can think about is the future. I want my heart to beat for something more, something magical. "And I want our son–"

"Or daughter," she interrupts.

I smile. "*Yes*, or daughter." I stick my tongue out at her and she swats my shoulder. I laugh. "I want our son *or daughter* to grow up knowing that their parents never stopped going on adventures. Like the old couple we saw at the tiny, beat up, old lighthouse. What a story it would be to tell our kids!"

She laughs. "It would be a good one, I guess."

"No! No guessing. No thinking. No worrying. The future is ours, Liz. And it's time we took control for once."

"Alright," she says. "Alright, let's do it!"

"Hallelujah," I say, sweeping her into my arms and kissing her like it's the end of the world. But then, it is. It's the end of the world as we know it. And something new is on its way.

55

I was never a good Christian.

Honestly, this isn't a new revelation for me. I've always known that when it comes to peoples' ideas of what a good Christian looks like I don't even come close. I'm what my Mom would call a bit of a prodigal. It's not something I'm proud of and it certainly isn't something I embrace, but it's something that just is. For now, anyway.

But something changed inside of me. Perhaps that's what happens when you stare death in the face. It's like all the hard places of my heart - all the thorny, dry places - have somehow opened up. I know I've still got a long way to go, but I was always taught to believe in a God who's present, who's beside you through everything. For so long, I was convinced that if God was real, then He'd abandoned me. But now a part of me is starting to wonder if maybe He's been there this whole time. Maybe He was letting some things in my life fall apart so that He could build something so much bigger and better.

Maybe...

If believing in God is about following a set of rules, then I don't want it. If heaven is real, I don't want to get there just because I managed to follow all the rules perfectly. I want it to mean something. I have no interest in a dead faith. There are already too many so-called Christians whose entire lives are a lie because they think that somehow, if they abstain from enough bad things or do enough good things then they can get to heaven.

If I'm going to believe in the impossible, I need it to come alive inside of me. I need it be real. I need it to mean something.

So, yeah, I may be a prodigal, but I like to think that maybe I'm making my way back. To what? I don't know. Something bigger, maybe. Something that goes beyond dead, dry religion - something *beautiful* and *new* and *exciting.* Something that makes me come alive.

I don't know if God even wants anything to do with me. I don't know if I'm worth forgiveness or if healing is even possible. But something that Liz said in the hospital burns in my mind: *"Right now, we need impossible. That's the only way we're going to get through this. That's the only way we're going to heal. If impossible is what it takes, then I'm all in."*.

So if God is who He says He is, then I'm all in too. Because Liz is right. I need impossible.

And I'm ready for that adventure.

56

In Gus' driver seat, I wait for Liz as she gathers her things. There's a thrill of anticipation in my heart and I vow to never forget this feeling, to always remember the magic of new things, good things. I take notice of the way every old thing - every moment of the last three months - comes together to forge the way to our future. This adventure. This moment. All of the questions in my heart and the answers that are unfolding. All of the faith to believe in the impossible that I can muster. Every bit of it is a promise of things yet to come. And I don't know what the future holds. I know that there will be pain there. But I also know, even more deeply, that there will be purpose.

I always thought I was a hurricane - and maybe I still am - but I'm starting to think that's not a bad thing. Because I've always wanted to make waves. And you can't do that without the wind. The bigger the wind, the bigger the wave. So I guess that even though I'm a hurricane, Liz is the wind that moves me and we're making waves together. We're *living* because it's the only thing we know to do anymore. The sea is in our blood. It's who we are. And it doesn't matter if everything around us is okay because as long as we're together, pioneering our way through old and into the new... everything is beautiful.

I don't know if any of that even makes sense. I *feel* it

more than I know it and it's hard to articulate the things that you feel deep inside. But it doesn't have to make sense to anyone but me. And honestly, all the best things in life? They'll never make sense. They can't be bound by logic. Like love. Or passion. Or heaven. Or infinity.

It's all so impossible.

And that, I think, is the way it should be.

As I sit in the van alone, waiting for Liz, somebody walks up beside the driver's door and I turn to see Oliver staring down at me.

"You're leaving," he says, his voice flat.

I nod, my lips half parted, but silent.

"I don't know if Liz told you any of what I said when you were in the hospital, but I figured it would be better if it came from me anyway."

I don't move or say anything. Liz said he came to visit me when I was in my coma and she told me some of what he said, but she had trouble remembering all of it.

"I just wanted to say I'm sorry, Adam," he says and then he falls silent for a minute. He starts to leave, but then turns back. "I wouldn't blame you if you said no, but I would really like it if we could be friends again. Or, at least, if we could work toward that." He offers a hopeful smile.

And I smile back, my heart bursting because that's all I ever wanted. "I'd like that," I say.

He backs away, arms swinging at his sides. "Okay, then. Have a safe trip and... I'll see you around."

"Yeah. See you around, man." I nod and he nods back, then turns and walks away.

Just as Oliver disappears into the dorms, Liz slides open the back door and throws her things inside. She closes it and hops into the passenger seat.

"So," she says. "Where to now?"

57

Oregon.

I shift Gus into gear and roar out of the parking lot. Glancing into the rearview mirror, I offer a silent goodbye to the school I hope to one day forget. I hope to God that no one has as bad an experience at that school as I did. Because no one deserves that.

"If you were an animal, what would you be?" I ask, continuing our endless game of 20 Questions. The California landscape passes us in a blur as we leave it behind, racing with all our hearts into the New.

She scrunches up her face, thinking for a moment. "I don't know. I've never really thought about it. What do you think?"

"I think you'd be a butterfly. They represent transformation, change, renewal, lightness of being, elevation from earthly matters and tuning into emotional or spiritual matters, and the world of the soul. So you're a butterfly."

She smiles. "I like that. What about you?"

"I'd be a wolf."

She raises an eyebrow at me and I laugh.

"It's true. The wolf is intelligent, has an appetite for freedom, expresses strong instincts, and is loyal, but when threatened, forms a lack of trust in someone or itself."

"Yeah, you'd definitely be a wolf. I don't think I've heard a more accurate description of your personality," she says with a laugh.

I smile.

"How do you know all this stuff?"

Sighing, I tighten my grip on the steering wheel. "I spent a long time not knowing who I was. After everything happened, I was lost and confused. I felt like I was just floating, a phantom with no solid grasp on my identity. So I did everything I could to define myself. I know that Christians are supposed to define themselves as God defines them, but that was always hard for me. I can't feel that, y'know? So I learned everything I could about my spirit animal, my Myers-Briggs Personality Type, my astrological sign – Taurus, by the way – and my bloodline."

"Has it helped at all?"

"Somewhat. A lot of those things I didn't realize the accuracy of until I started living again." I glance over at Liz. "You helped me learn to live again, Liz."

She smiles and I turn back to the road.

"And now I know that my spirit animal doesn't matter. And my astrological sign doesn't matter. And my personality type doesn't matter. Those are just labels. And while they helped me ground myself at the time, they didn't help me learn to live. Only you did that.

"Jeremiah told me once that I depended too much on him and that I needed to learn to depend on God for everything because 'people will fail you'. And he let that be his excuse for so long. But the thing is, man wasn't born to live life completely isolated and independent from other people. Man was born for love and happiness and community. I may be mistaken, but didn't God say 'It is not good for man to be alone?' I just don't get how people can underestimate the power of relationships." I pause. "People like me and you spend so long feeling alone and isolated already that, sometimes, we're too open to accept people into our lives just to feel that sense of togetherness, to feel like we're not alone. And then those people end up betraying us and we're alone again. Maybe some people aren't built to handle hurricanes. Maybe it takes a special type of person – like you, Liz – a storm-chaser, someone who's built for it."

She stops me then. "I don't believe that for a second. Because if that's true, that means that people can just keep making the same excuse: 'I'm not the right person for you. You need to find someone who can handle your mess.' Life and people shouldn't be allowed to work that way."

"You're right," I say. "They shouldn't. But we can't control them. What we *can* do is make choices every day to step toward healing. To get the help we need, to confide in someone, to be honest, to be brave. Little by little, step by step, we'll make it. You and me? We'll make it."

I glance at Liz beside me. She just sits there, in the passenger seat, a smile on her face as she stares out the windshield at the road ahead. And, for the first time in my life, I realize I'm happy. And I realize how strong I am – how strong Liz made me. And I hope I've made her stronger too.

So much has happened these last few months. All the hurt, all the pain, all the grief and the trauma that had been stirring inside of me for so long... it's all been poured out now and I can't take it back. I glance at Liz and I realize that she was not immune to the things I'd suffered. I pushed her. I hurt her. And I almost left her alone to bear the burden of our foolishness on her own.

"Liz," I say... She looks at me, brow furrowed. "I'm so sorry."

"For what?" she asks.

"For hurting you." I clear my throat. "For pushing you. For leaving you. It wasn't right or fair. It was selfish and I'm so, so, deeply sorry."

She smiles, eyes watering. "I forgive you, Adam. I'll always forgive you." She pauses. "Adam, I love you and I want you to know that I'll always be there for you just like I know you'll be there for me. But the thing is that we can't be each other's source. You and I, the love that we share, it helps. It's important. It mends and it heals. But it isn't enough. One day, we're gonna mess up again and when that happens we need to be able to hold ourselves together. We can't be so dependent on each other that when we mess up, we destroy each other. It's no secret that we're both deeply flawed."

I don't know why, but I laugh at that.

She smiles too. "Adam, I can't be your answer. I can't be your source. Don't get me wrong. I'll do what's mine to do. I'll love you and I'll walk beside you through everything. But I've been realizing recently that I can't carry you. Not on my own, anyway. It's sad, but people just aren't built to bear that kind of weight. We're inherently weak. We can try, but we'll fall short. A lot." She breathes out a sigh as I listen quietly. "There's something inside of yourself that you're going to have to access in order to fully heal. I'll never be enough. Adam, your faith cannot be in me because I will *fail* you. And I'll hate it then just like I hate it now, but it's inevitable. And you will fail me too. So there has to be more to us than just you and me because we're not enough and that's okay." She reaches over and grabs my hand. "But I promise – I *promise* from the deepest parts of who I am – that I will be your home. But I can't be your healing. You're going to have to find that for yourself."

"I know," I say. Everything she said echoes inside of my spirit and I know in my heart of hearts that she's right. "I've struggled with that for a long time, but I think that, deep down, I've always known that." I smile at her, reassuring her. "I want you to promise me something," I say, my eyes steady on the road ahead, my fingers loose around the steering wheel as night begins to fall, lit only by the city lights. She looks over at me, her eyes radiant.

"What?" she asks.

"After this trip, I want you to promise me that you'll pursue legal action against your uncle." I glance over at her to see her mouth hang open.

"Adam, I-"

"Look, Liz... I don't know what it's like. I know that it must be scary, but take it from me. You'll never be able to move past it until you confront it. I learned that the hard way." I glance at my wrists, at the scars still fresh and red from the stitches. "Promise me, Liz." I glance over at her again. "I'll be right there by your side through the whole thing. Me and our baby. You won't be alone."

She thinks for a minute, staring through the windshield out at the road. "Okay," she sighs after a while.

I smile over at her. "Okay." Reaching over, I take her hand in mine and hold it for a long time.

58

As the night carries on, I pull off to the side of the road along Exit 11 somewhere outside of the Klamath National Forest. This feeling that I've been here before washes over me. Under a blanket of deep blue, I remember the moments all those weeks ago when Liz and I pulled off of the road and just lay on the ground, watching the stars in the middle of the Nevada desert.

Desperate for the nostalgia, I get out and grab a blanket out of the trunk. I circle around the van and spread the blanket atop the grassy knoll that separates the exit from the main road. Liz follows me out and we lie down on the blanket together, staring up at the still blue. The sky is clear tonight and the evening wind is cool and crisp, but not cold. The stars are brilliant against the deep, black universe.

"It's like magic," she says. "The night is so dark and so many fear it, but you look up and there they are, the stars standing like watchmen over the sleepers."

"It's perfect," I say. I move my hand and touch my fingertips to Liz's. I let them stay there for a second. Slowly, I slide my hand into hers, stroking the space between her thumb and index finger. I smile up at the sky. "The night is dark, but we are not." The array of colors burns itself into my eyes and I don't know what it is I feel, but I almost want to cry. It isn't sadness or pain, but a still unfamiliar feeling that might almost be peace or happiness.

Liz rolls over to face me. She props her head up in the palm of her hand. I turn my head and stare at her. I can't take my eyes off of her.

"You're so beautiful," I say. I realize I haven't said those words to her in a long time. Now, though, it's like I have no choice. Hers is a beauty that demands attention.

It's dark, but under the moonlight I can see that she is blushing. I lean in to kiss her because sometimes words aren't enough to express a feeling. And right now I feel her, right here next to me. I feel her heart beating next to mine and I feel the heartbeat of our child inside of her. It's so beautifully imperfect how every scar on my body and every wound in her heart have come together to create a future for both of us.

I pull away and roll onto my side, resting my head on my arm. With my free hand, I trace every curve of her face, my thumb pressing gently against the dimple beside her lips. "I'm not going to say you're perfect because you would know that's a lie and I don't ever want to lie to you. And let's be honest... we're a mess." We laugh. "But the thing is, we don't have to be perfect and we don't have to hide that." I pause, losing myself in the deep blue of her eyes. "Liz, you mend me."

Liz smiles at me and she laughs as she brings her hands to my face and holds me between her palms. "We mend each other," she says, eyes swimming.

I smile as she pulls my lips to meet hers and we kiss under the starlight.

59

The scenery changes from dry hills to lush mountain forests quickly as we drive deep into the heart of Oregon. The rain pours outside, heavy and cold. I turn the heat up and the windows fog so Liz wipes them clear with her sleeve every now and then.

"I love the rain," I say.

She smiles over at me. "I know you do."

Her words warm my depths, knowing that there is someone who finally knows the heart of me. I've given all of me to her and I don't regret one moment of it.

We drive and drive as the hours pass and the weather changes and the landscape grows greener and more vibrant, the colors of spring filling its voids and the melting snow filling its rivers. Liz digs around in the truck for my camera and, finding the bag, she pulls it out, removing the lens cap. She rolls down the window, ignoring the rain drops that fall inside, drenching the inside of her door and her arms, and she takes pictures of the world as we pass it. Fog ascends from the earth as the rain waters it. The trees seem a darker green than even possible and they follow every swell of the hills as they grow from knolls into mountains, grasping at the grey.

Liz takes picture after picture, leaning out the window into the rain until the entire upper half of her body is out among the elements and through the wind and the rain I hear her laughing. She slides back inside and sits down and I glance over to see that she is soaking wet, but she doesn't care. Her hair sticks to her face and her clothes cling to her skin. She turns the camera to me and I smile at her as she takes the picture. She sets the camera down in the console, rolls up her window, and crawls into the back. In the rearview mirror, I watch her as she uses one of the blankets to dry herself off and then changes out of her wet clothes.

The rain doesn't let up by the time we reach Multnomah Falls at around 4:30 in the evening. We pull into the parking spot and through the trees, I see the distant falls, crashing against the mountain wall. It's still raining, but only lightly by now. Pulling my denim jacket on, I hop out of the van. I walk over to the passenger side and open the door for Liz as she puts her own jacket on. She hangs my camera around her neck, steps out into the rain, and stands on the tip of her toes, leaning into me. I wrap my arms around her and give her a kiss, smiling into her lips. She tucks her hands into my chest and I move her to the side so I can close her door.

Hand in hand, we walk across the parking lot and find the hiking trail. We're all but shielded from the rain by the trees around us as their branches sprawl and tangle high above, forming a natural canopy. We follow the trail until we come to the bridge that passes in front of the waterfall. Stopping halfway across the bridge, I'm thankful that we're the only ones here right now.

I lean against the railing and face the waterfall, letting the mist wash over every part of me, cleansing me and it feels so good. Turning to Liz, I swoop her into my arms, and kiss her deeply in the middle of the mist and the rain.

My world is spinning and my head is throbbing and my heart is racing. Moments like this are so rare and so perfect and I don't ever want to let it go, so I just kiss Liz as if my life depends on it, because I think that maybe it does. I would be a fool to think that I could ever survive on my own. No one is built to try to live life on their own. No one.

So I cling to her and she clings to me under the weight of the sky. No one else is here, so we stay like this for a moment longer, lingering above the clouds, away from the scrutiny of the world.

Pulling away, our eyes linger in the space between our bodies as we stare at each other. I move my hand to feel her belly, where our baby grows with every passing second. I kiss her again, but on the forehead this time. "I love you, Liz."

"I love you too, Adam."

I smile as I pull my camera over her neck I move over to the opposite railing and set the camera down, aiming it toward the waterfall, toward us. I set the timer and walk back over to Liz, pulling her into my arms. "I don't ever want to forget this moment," I say, aware of the slow ten-second countdown.

8...

"I don't ever want to forget this feeling."

6...

"I don't ever want to forget what the world was like when

it was just me and you above it all."

3...

"So kiss me like it's all we have."

1...

She wraps her arms around me and pulls my lips to hers and we kiss because this is our moment. This is our time.

In the distance, I hear the click of the camera.

60

I have to fight the fears. They are ruthless in their pursuit of my sanity.

As we drive away from Multnomah Falls, our route set for Canon Beach, Liz naps and I'm left alone with my fears. I don't know how my mind can be so overwhelmed by my fears only moments after feeling so alive and so free. But I will be strong.

I *am* strong. It's who I am and I won't ever let anything change that.

I don't know what to do and with Liz asleep, I have no one to talk to. Even if she was awake, I wouldn't know what to say. I feel so responsible for her and I'm afraid to say anything that might cause her to doubt me because I want to be strong for her.

I will be strong.

So I do something I haven't done in a long time. There's no real reason for it and I don't even know if it will work; it feels so foreign. But despite all that, I say to myself, *God, make me brave.*

Because I refuse to live in a world where I'm afraid all the time. I refuse to live in a world of "what-ifs" and second-guessing. I refuse to live in a world where my past keeps me from living.

Glancing over at Liz as she sleeps, I smile to myself

because I remember how perfectly imperfect she is too. She has fears too. She has insecurities too. I'm not some special case that my fears are somehow more important or deadly than hers.

And I remember how strong she is and how far she's come – how far we've both come.

She is the sun and I am the moon and the night is dark, but we are not.

We are bright.

We are brave.

61

My phone tells me it's 7 PM as I pull into the parking lot of Canon Beach. Liz has been awake for a while now and when I turn Gus off, we just sit in the van for a few minutes, watching the ocean in the distance. Moonlight spills through the fog and onto the waves, illuminating every fracture of the sea.

Smiling, I look to Liz. "Come on," I say. Opening the door, I jump out of the van. Stripping down to my boxers, I walk toward the ocean. The sound of the crashing waves overwhelms me and my heart races against my chest, beating against this prison of flesh and bone.

Liz's bare feet slap against the sand as she follows me and I don't turn around because I feel the call of the sea as if it were calling me home. I can't stop myself. The cold air wisps across my chest, scattering goosebumps over my skin, but I ignore its bite. The wind picks up and in the distance I see the silhouette of Haystack Rock, a long shadow cast across the ocean and the shore as they meet. My hair flies with the wind, wild and unrestrained, subject to the currents of the atmosphere around me.

I don't stop when my feet hit the icy waves and I keep walking, deeper and deeper, further and further until the water is up to my chest and I'm swimming. It's dangerous, I know, but I really, really don't care. I let the waves wash over me and when I hear Liz splashing through the waves behind me, I turn around as she swims up to me. Her teeth chatter, but she's smiling.

"You do know we're neither sea creatures, nor nocturnal creatures, right?"

I grin. "We are what we are."

She laughs. The moon shines down on her like a spotlight, illuminating every curve and line.

"You're so beautiful," I say, tucking the loose strands of her hair behind her ears. I swim in the brilliant blue of her eyes, lost at sea, lost in her.

She smiles gently at me, lips trembling with every shiver of her body.

"I want to be honest with you, Liz."

She furrows her brow at me, blinking.

"Can we do that? Can we be honest?"

"Yes," she says, pressing her hand to my cheek, wiping away a drip of water as it trails down the side of my face.

"I'm afraid, Liz."

"Afraid of what?"

"That I won't be good enough for you. That I won't be good enough for our kid. That I'll relapse and hurt you or myself. I want to be good enough, Liz. I want to give you the life you deserve."

"Adam," she whispers. "You have always been – and will always be – more than good enough for me. Neither of us is perfect and we'll make mistakes – lots of them – but we'll learn from them. We'll fight and we'll have our good days and our bad days, but we'll never stop loving each other because a love like ours doesn't just fade away. It's timeless and it endures because that's who we are." She rests her arms on my shoulders and toys with the hair at the nape of my neck, twirling it around her fingers. "So don't ever be afraid that you're not good enough for me because I'll tell you right now that you are. And don't ever stop being honest with me because the moment that you do is the moment a wall forms between us and I don't want there to be any walls. I want all of you, every part, forever."

"Promise?" I whisper. We're a breath away from each other now.

"Promise," she whispers back.

I smile at her. "I have something for you." I open my fist to show her what I've been gripping onto and I hold it between us, watching the way the dusk dances across the golden band. The diamond sparkles like starlight between us and her eyes widen. Her mouth drops open slightly, but she doesn't say anything.

"My mom gave this to me when I left for college. She told me that I would find someone, someday, who would matter to me more deeply than any person ever has before," I say, staring down at the ring. "*You* are my someone. *You* are my someday." I pause, inhaling the salty air. "Liz, will you marry me?"

"Yes," she whispers.

I lean into her, wrapping my arms around her, pulling her soul into mine and we kiss under the light of a billion suns.

I hear everything all at once as the world spins without

us. She is the sea and I am the shore, lost in her depths once more. We sway with every wave and we live inside the currents of the wind and of the sea. We are hopelessly, desperately lost within each other as the stars sing their song around us and the wind carves its path across the deep, blue sky and the fog buries itself in the sea. We thrive above it all.

We are the ocean in a breath.

We are endless.

DEAR READER,

This story isn't perfect. Honestly, even if I was capable of writing the perfect story, I don't know that I would want to... because, then, it wouldn't be real. The only thing I ever want to do is be real.

Stories like these are hard to write because there is a certain weight to them. As an author, there's this understanding of the responsibility I have to portray things like mental illness, sexual assault, or abortion in a balanced and empathetic way. I hope that, with this story, I succeeded.

Within these pages, you met Adam. You met a young man who was broken, who was tired of fighting to survive the war that raged within his mind, who was tired of remembering all the painful things that had happened to him. A young man who was abused and betrayed and who couldn't see past himself. And you met Liz, a young woman with a lot of hope and a light in her eyes, but who soon discovered that you can't fully heal when you ignore what's hurting you. Adam and Liz are two people whose views of life were, at times, polar opposite. One was full of light and the other couldn't see his way through the dark.

My hope in writing *Love and the Sea* was that, for those of you who may see a little bit of yourself in either Adam or

Liz, you might come to realize one thing: there is hope. You may not know it, believe it, or feel it right now, but you could be just one breath away from your moment. You could be one step away from healing and freedom from your pain. You could be one kind word away from belonging. You could be just one daring, foolish prayer away from resurrection.

And wherever you are, whatever has happened to you... there is a light brighter than belief. Even if you can't see your way through the dark right now, the light is coming. It won't be easy and it's going to take all of your strength, but one day you'll remember all the decisions and moments that, little by little, brought you back to life. And, even though it hurt at times, you won't regret it. Not one bit. Trust me. Because I've been in the lowest valley surrounded by the deep, deep dark, struggling to make the choices that I could only hope would lead me out. And I've also been on the highest mountain, looking back down at that valley, remembering who I used to be and seeing what those daring and foolishly hopeful choices have made me into. And I look back, too, and see where Jesus was standing beside me the whole time, holding me up and fighting for me, like a friend who never left, a brother-in-arms who fights to the death.

You are not what happened to you. You are not the things that you feel. You are not the way people treat you, the names they call you, or the labels they thrust upon you. But you are the choices that you make. To heal. To open up. To dare to dream, to hope, to have faith. Even if it's the last thing you do. Even if you've run out of options. Even if it hurts. Even if you're the only one. Believe me: it's worth it.

So open up. Let the light in.
Brian McBride

ACKNOWLEDGEMENTS

This story has been a long time in the making. Finishing it wouldn't have been possible without a handful of special people. First, I'd like to thank my parents, Mark & Debra McBride, for your constant and endless support, for your unconditional love, for fighting for me and believing in me.

Thank you to my grandparents, Loren, Esther, Fred, and Marilyn, who've gifted me with so much wisdom, insight, and guidance.

Thank you to my brother and sister, Michael and Eden, and to my cousins, Christopher and Tehilla, for being my closest friends, for being people I can always count on, and for being people I can always be myself around.

Thank you to to all my writer friends who have been there through my journey as a writer and with this story in ways big and small: Olivia Bennett, Sierra Abrams, Victoria Gaytan, Sahara Moran, Liz Brooks, Marjolein Ribberink, Maddy Wilson, Leah Oxendine, Mirriam Neal, Caroline Meek, and Kara Swanson.

Lastly, from the deepest parts of my heart, I'm endlessly grateful to my Savior. You saw me when I was at my lowest and You weren't afraid to get down in the dirt with me. You believed in me more than anyone. You saw every dark and broken part of my heart and filled the fractures with Your endless light. Every single day, You make me come alive. There's no one like You. My heart is Yours. My world is Yours.

ABOUT THE AUTHOR

A winner of the 2016 Wattys Award, Brian published the award-winning Young Adult Contemporary debut, Love and the Sea and Everything in Between, in 2018.

Born and raised in Oregon, Brian moved to California at sixteen, where he has lived ever since. He's been writing since he was thirteen-years-old and has been reading for longer. Brian is pursuing a degree in Social Work, which he hopes to use to aid children and families. Perhaps he'll work to better the United States foster care system. Or maybe he'll join an organization that fights human trafficking. A fourth generation pastor and founder of the Pioneer Movement, he is passionate about his faith and longs to see Christians become all that they are called to be. Among other things, he is also passionate about iced tea, animals, adoption, and the arts.

INSTAGRAM - @brianmcbrideauthor
WEBSITE – www.brianalexandermcbride.com
FACEBOOK – www.facebook.com/brianmcbrideauthor

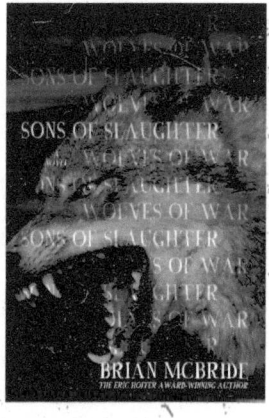

www.ingramcontent.com/pod-product-compliance
Lightning Source LLC
Chambersburg PA
CBHW020343180626
46812CB00001B/313